CW00705662

STEPHANI

THE REAPER

CHILDREN OF WISDOM · BOOK 2

Reap what you sow, dear reader.

ONE

"The humans are fragile, and therefore must be handled with care. To effectively help them transition from their world to the next, the Reaper must know when to use a gentle touch, and when to use a firm hand."
—*Mortem, Section 1, Paragraph 1: On Reapers*

The mists between our worlds are thick and tempestuous today, and given all the rules I've just broken, it seems like an ominous sign. Even though I've already traveled back and forth through the mists several hundred times, I can't afford to lose my concentration yet, not when there's one name left on my list. It's time for me to head to Colorado to claim the soul of Dempsey Shellman. Still, I can't deny my thoughts are more with my friend Penn, the banished Fate, than they are with poor Dempsey.

Before a human is born, the Fates determine what type of person he will be, how long he will live, and how he will die. His path is set out before him, and he cannot divert from it. So, while being a Reaper is not exactly easy, it is usually predictable. We only take souls that are, literally, at the end of their rope… or, well, the end of the thread the Spinner has created for them. But not long ago, surprises started popping up on our lists. Souls who weren't supposed to take the journey to the afterlife for decades were showing up without apparent reason.

It's an anomaly the Reapers have no idea how to stop, which is why I have risked Penn's very existence by cutting his banishment short. We need all the help we can get, and I'm not sure I can figure this out without him. Despite the fact that he was banished for the distractions his love for a human created, he's still the greatest Fate in history. It's that connection to the human that will drive him to help me figure out what's happening, and why she and the others ended up dying before their time.

I shake my head in an attempt to clear it. Dwelling on the surprise deaths won't help me get Dempsey where he needs to go. I will deal with the mystery later, once the workday is over.

As the mists clear on a busy downtown street in Denver, I'm left standing in front of a ten-story office building. The sun is gloriously warm on my skin, but the air still has a bit of a chill to it, making the sun feel even more welcome on this lovely spring day. I take in a deep breath, letting myself enjoy the scent of the clean mountain air, all the more delightful because it's in the middle of the city.

The building is modern on the inside, decorated in greys and blacks with a few red accent pieces—a rug here, an abstract painting there. I stride across the lobby, unnoticed by the receptionist and the people milling about, and board the elevator just as a few others are getting off. Happily, someone else on this floor happens to be going up to the eighth floor as well. That's where I know I'll find him. The man reaches out and presses the button for eight, paying me no mind.

His office is along the back wall, with a maze of cubicles in the center of the large room. He's one of the only people with actual walls and windows. The sounds of frantic clicking and typing, phones ringing, and hushed conversation follow me as I make my way across the floor. Not one person looks up from their work to look at me, nor should they. I'm not here for them.

One woman who's on the phone looks up just as I walk past her cubicle. She stares right at me, but her vacant expression confirms that she doesn't see me. I often wonder what makes some humans look up as I pass them, while others don't react to my presence at all. Do I create a gentle breeze? Are some humans simply more attuned to our world? It's a question that may never be answered. The woman goes back to her conversation, and I keep walking to the back of the floor, making my way toward my quarry.

When I walk into his office, the middle-aged man I've come to collect is yelling at a young woman. Dempsey Shellman is a big man, overweight and balding. Despite the fact that he's visibly sweating, not to mention spitting with every word he yells, he's intimidating. He's still wearing his black suit coat, which isn't helping his sweat situation. The woman, who's probably half his age, stands there listening to him. She writes down any instructions she can pick out between his insults, but I can tell she's on the verge of tears. Her hatred for the man radiates from her.

"Dempsey," I say to the man. "It's time to go."

He clears his throat and pounds his chest a little, ignoring me. I know I will win in the end—I always do—so I wait patiently. He will struggle, and it won't be pretty for this young girl. I want her to leave. But she stands there without flinching.

"I don't know who you slept with to get your job, but you are the most worthless assistant I've ever…" He trails off, his breath coming in short gasps now. Bracing himself on the desk with one hand, he grabs his chest with the other.

"Mr. Shellman?" the young woman asks, clearly unsure of what's happening.

"Are you ready now?" I ask.

Finally, he looks at me. His face has lost its color, and his eyes are filled with terror. I attempt to calm him.

"My name is Michaela. I'm a Reaper. I'm here to take you home." The mists are gathering behind me, telling me it's time to go, and I gesture toward it, trying to show him. The breeze from it ruffles my black-and-white gown, tossing my long, blonde hair around my face. Some of the humans I collect mistake me for an angel, but there's one key difference—I don't have wings.

The man still doesn't respond. He slumps in his chair before sliding grotesquely to the ground. The poor girl screams and runs out of Dempsey's office, calling for help as she goes. But it's his time, and he's beyond their help. His soul, a carbon copy of his body, looks back as it raises from his Earthly self. They don't all look back, but I can tell this one is very rooted in the world—taking him will be a struggle. He's a lot larger than I am, and I can only hope it's not the black gate that appears for him. But based on what little I've seen of him, let's just say I'm a bit concerned.

If he has questions, he doesn't vocalize them. As I wait for him to join me, it occurs to me that I will not be very efficient today. This one will be time consuming, but that's okay. Some people need more of me than others do. It's all part of the job. Reapers are trained to be exactly what the humans we collect need us to be.

While I wait for him to come to terms with his fate, people rush into the office and try to help.

"He's not breathing," one man says. They start pounding on his chest while the young girl—apparently Dempsey's assistant—stands in the doorway watching, relaying information to a person she's talking to on her cell phone. Probably a 911 operator.

"He just grabbed his chest and slumped over," she says. "They said he's not breathing." Pause. "Okay."

A few others crowd along the walls of the office, not sure what to do. A man and a woman lean toward each other to speculate on what happened. "Think it was a heart attack?" the man asks.

"I'm not sure. Do you think he'll be okay?" she asks. It's hard to tell from their short exchange, but it sounds like she's more upset by the horror of what's happened than by the fact that it's happened to Dempsey.

"He looks a little blue," the man says as he shifts his weight, clearly uncomfortable. He leans in a little closer to the woman. Their coworkers can't hear him now, but *we* can. "I won't lie. I've been hoping he would leave. God, we all were… just not this way. I didn't want the S.O.B. to die."

Confusion blooms on Dempsey's face. He's only now realizing how much they hate him. It's sad, really—especially now that he can't hope to change things for the better—and I reach out my hand to him.

"Come, Dempsey. There's nothing more for you to see here."

Stoically, he nods his head and walks toward me. He resists holding my hand though, which is problematic. His only way through the mists is with me, and I can't leave him here. If I do, he'll become a ghost—doomed to wander the Earth forever. The few ghosts I've had to leave behind over the centuries still haunt me in their own way. No matter how bleak a human's soul, I won't leave one behind if I can help it.

"You need to hold my hand. It's the only way through the mists," I tell him.

Dempsey looks at me with disgust, like holding my hand is the most deplorable thing he's ever been asked to do. I take a deep breath, reminding myself to be what he needs. And right now, he needs to make the journey between worlds safely.

Because he is so attached to the Earth, I resist telling him what will happen to him if he doesn't take my hand. I just stand there, waiting for him to decide. Fortunately, he takes my hand on his own, and we begin to walk through the mists, which closes in around us with every step. He looks back several times, trying desperately to hang on to that life—to the power and position he clearly attained. But I keep him moving forward, one step at a time.

I'm curious about what his memories will reveal about him. Every human I take to the other side relives their pivotal moments—the ones that have shaped them into who they are today—as we walk through the mists separating Earth from the heavens. Dempsey is no exception.

As his memories start to play, I watch them right alongside him. The first ones are from when he was young. His mother yelling at him, telling him she wished he'd never been born. Blaming his existence for her unhappiness over and over again. The repeated verbal lashings and manipulations turned him cold and hard. By the time he reached adulthood, he kept his distance from everyone. No dating, no friends, and no close family. Just him.

I glance over to gauge his reaction to these harsh memories. His face is briefly twisted in a flash of pain, but the emotion disappears in an instant, leaving behind a stony, unemotional expression in its wake.

As we continue our walk down memory lane, as it were, I see that his self-induced isolation was the secret to his success. However, he didn't come by all of his accomplishments honestly. He liked to take shortcuts where he could. After all, why work harder when a shorter route would get you to the same objective?

The deeper we go into the mists, the darker the memories get. I see him fire hard-working family men without blinking so he can bring on cheaper, younger workers and interns to do the same jobs—a decision he refers to as "smart business sense." I watch him cut corners, take credit for others' work, and hurt person after person, all in the name of moving up the corporate ladder.

Chancing a glance over at him, my fears are confirmed. He's smiling. He's proud of these memories.

Finally, after an exhausting walk, we come to his last memory, his most defining moment. This is the one that will show me which gate to expect at the end of the mists. If his memory is happy and loving, I will know that, despite his sins, he's earned a place in heaven. If not, the black gate will be waiting for us.

Despite the fact that not one of his memories was happy, I still hold out hope for this man. When the Fates spin a life for their tapestry, the color of the thread reflects the type of person he or she will become. Greys are an odd breed—some are good, some are bad, but they're never wholly so, which makes it difficult to predict where they'll end up after death. Dempsey is clearly a grey thread, a man who regularly walked the line of moral ambiguity, but it's not an automatic go-directly-to-jail card. Greys can still go to heaven.

His final memory forms in front of us on the mists, playing out like a movie on a giant projection screen. I cling to his hand in anticipation, but he lets his fingers dangle loosely in my grip.

I watch him sitting in a dark office. It seems to be after hours. A large executive desk separates him from another man with dark hair so slicked back it's shiny. Dempsey is young in this memory, perhaps in his late twenties. The thin, secondhand suit he's wearing doesn't quite fit him right, but he's paired it with a nice silver statement tie, probably to distract from the poor quality and fit. It tells me he hasn't come into his money yet, but he doesn't want people to know it.

"If we do this, and someone finds out, we could go to jail," the man says.

"If we do this and succeed, we'll be promoted to the top positions in the company," young Dempsey says. The look on his face tells me he's excited, even exhilarated. I frown and look over at the man next to me. A smile tugs at the corners of his mouth, telling me he enjoys this memory.

"A lot of people will go bankrupt for this. Lives will be ruined. I can think of a few who might even kill themselves," the greasy-haired man says.

Young Dempsey shrugs and leans back in the chair across the desk from the man, clearly not as concerned as his coworker is. "Less competition, if you ask me."

"Riding out the panic will be key."

"Starting the panic will be the fun part," Dempsey says with what sounds like glee.

"You are a bit disturbing, Dempsey." Although the man looks untrustworthy in every way—salt-and-pepper hair slicked back with grease, pointed features that make him look like a super villain when he smiles, and an overly starched suit that makes him look like a used car salesman—I can't help but agree with him.

"Not disturbing. Successful. There's a difference."

"Is there?" the older man asks.

Dempsey chuckles. But the sound isn't happy or contagious like it sometimes is when people laugh. No, his chuckle is more of a derisive snort that leaves an ugly feeling in the pit of my stomach. "No, maybe not."

And that's it—that's where it ends. I don't know the outcome of their plot, let alone the specifics of what they did. I suspect they orchestrated some stock market crash that earned them millions. I'm not sure it's enough for the black gate. I hope it isn't, but I fear it might be. He was too happy about it, too carefree about the consequences. They love the selfish in hell, and Dempsey here is one of the most selfish men I've ever reaped.

As the mists clear, I hold my breath. The man stands next to me, relaxed, but I brace myself for what's coming. Very few souls accept their fate willingly when it comes to hell. And this man doesn't seem like he's used to consequences.

Much to my chagrin, my fears are confirmed, and the black gate appears on the other side of the mists, but there's no sign of the demons that are usually are there to collect the souls of the doomed. I cling to Dempsey's hand, holding tight. Where are they? I have been a Reaper for many centuries, and never have the demons missed the opportunity to collect a soul. Their absence is yet another sign that the usual rules no longer apply.

On instinct, the man tries to jerk away from me as soon as he sees the gate. It looms over us, threatening to suck all the happiness from our lives.

"No," Dempsey says. It's the first word he's spoken since we met. Even without any sign of the demons, he knows. It's impossible not to—the gate practically emanates the worst emotions humans feel. His eyes grow wide and dart around, searching desperately for a way out.

Now's my chance, while he's in shock. If I wait, he'll really start fighting me. I hate to see them fight. It always breaks my heart.

I've never been in this situation before. The demons are *always* here, so combative humans are their problem. I don't like to watch the struggle, so I tend to disappear back into the mists, hoping the next soul on my list will meet a better fate.

I pull Dempsey along as he stares slack jawed at the beauty and horror that is the black gate of hell. Thankfully, he follows me automatically… for now, at least. The tortured forms of the humans who came before him are carved into the black stone—

all are crying, and all are doomed for eternity. I imagine it must be a terrible thing to try to comprehend, especially moments after his unexpected demise.

As I push the gate open, he finally starts to pull away, and my heart cries for him. His fight is futile, of course. As a spirit, he's lost his physical heft and strength.

"Come on now. Don't fight me, please."

"Why? So you can toss me into the pit of hell? I don't think so." And just like that, he pulls back his free hand and tries to punch me in the face. It's a ridiculous move. Even if he makes contact with me, I won't feel anything. But the intent behind it shows me his soul is even darker than I'd thought.

It makes something inside of me snap—this man who's hurt so many people is trying to hurt me—and suddenly, I'm out of patience. I yank him through the gate with little sympathy. It's the first time I've ever done anything like that. Centuries ago, when I was first training to be a Reaper, we were taught to always be compassionate with the humans, even those who possessed the blackest of souls. But this man rubs me the wrong way, and I start to wonder about myself. Have I been a Reaper too long? Am I losing my touch?

I've always been a bit… eccentric for a Reaper, drawn more to the company of the Fates than that of my own kind. That's not to say I'm not friendly with the other Reapers, but the Fates have always interested me more. I'm drawn to their creations, their processes, and their love for each other. Sometimes, I think I should've been a Fate, but their jobs are just as hard, and occasionally as heart wrenching, as mine. I shake my head. Despite my lack of compassion for the soul in front of me, I know I'm doing the work I'm meant to do.

After the gate closes behind us, I straighten and glare at Dempsey's soul, anger bubbling deep inside of me. It's not an emotion I feel very often, but this man is about to get the full force of it.

I narrow my eyes at him. "If you ever try a move like that again," I say, keeping my voice low and even, "I will personally see to it that the demons have an extra-special reason to torture you. Let me tell you, the demons here like their jobs. They don't need a reason to make your life more miserable, but if I give them one, they'll be happy to oblige."

His face goes white, but I can tell the fight hasn't gone out of him. Not giving him time to think, I guide him deeper into the depths of hell, trying to hide my desperate search for a demon to take him from me. If I make him think this is normal, I have an advantage. If he sees my desperation, I'll end up chasing after him for half the night. Definitely not my idea of a good time.

More than once, he tries to run, and more than once, I consider letting him. Now that he's on the other side of the gate, he can't escape. The gates only open from the inside for heavenly beings, not human souls. That's true for heaven too. We don't want lost souls wandering around. Once they reach their new home, they're there for good. Still, I go after him each time he tries to flee, determined to do my job even if the demons aren't doing theirs. I'm not going to let him wander around hell before he's properly processed.

Finally, I find a pair of Torturers. They aren't my first pick. Guardians make an effort to follow the rules—as generalized as they are. They would at least process the soul—find out who they are and what they've done—*before* torturing him. But I have little choice. Although my workday is technically over, there is nothing I can do for this man's soul. Frankly, there is nothing I care to do. He's shown me his true nature, and I want no part of it. It's much more important for me to figure out what's going on in the heavens.

"Why are there no Guardians at the gates?" I demand.

The demons don't seem cowed. "How should we know, Reaper? We're not their keepers," one of them responds, its voice high and scratchy. Dempsey shrinks back from them, and rightfully so. Torturers are fluid in form. They change appearance to exploit their victims' greatest fears or desires. But they don't yet know Dempsey, so they appear as they always do— huge, black, and horned, with red eyes and razor-sharp claws. Anyone's nightmare.

"What do we have here?" the one on the left asks me.

"Your newest resident," I say with a hint of regret. Despite what he's done, it still saddens me to leave him here. It almost always does. *Almost.* There was one exception—a murderer who had a liking for children. I took quite a few of his victims to heaven before he was finally executed. He's one of the only souls I've reaped for whom I felt no empathy. I still don't.

"Wonderful." Dempsey recoils as two demons reach out for him with charred hands.

"They've been burned," he says, almost to himself.

I don't respond. He has a lot to learn about his new home, but he has an eternity to do it.

"I trust you'll take care of him properly," I say. It's not a question.

"You're a foolish one to put your trust in demons, Reaper," one of them says, his red eyes laughing at me. His sharp, yellowed teeth form a gruesome smile.

"Maybe," I say, but I leave it at that. I don't like to engage the demons in unnecessary conversation. It never ends well.

I have no closing words for Dempsey. No words of encouragement. *Nothing.* While he was reluctant to hold my hand before, now he clings to me, knowing what my departure will mean for him.

"I'm sorry," he screams, tears of desperation flowing freely down his cheeks.

"Me too," I say. With that, I shake my hand free, turn my back on him, and walk back toward the gate, leaving him to his eternal doom.

Hell is dark, filled with the stench of sulfur, rotting flesh, and other unpleasant things. No matter where you are inside the dark gate, your ears are assailed with the din of souls being tortured in unimaginable ways. Needless to say, I don't enjoy spending time here. Once I'm out of sight of the two demons and Dempsey, I hurry to leave as fast as my feet will carry me. But a sound stops me in my tracks before I reach the gate.

Someone's crying.

It's not an unusual sound to hear in hell. Plenty of souls cry out for help, and many others simply cry in their anguish. But I'm on the outskirts. The sound shouldn't be so pronounced this far from the torture chambers. I follow it around a few rocky turns, entering an area of hell I haven't visited before. It makes me a little nervous, and I take special care to notice landmarks that will help me find my way out. Hell is designed to keep its residents *inside*, and as such, it is a quagmire of caves and crevices all leading nowhere. Torches burn red against the walls, casting an eerie glow as I continue to follow the sound.

I finally reach a long, empty corridor. It's odd to find such a place in hell, particularly during working hours. During the day, there are usually demons wandering around everywhere except for the area directly around the gate. That same feeling of dread I had when I didn't see the Guardians outside the black gate washes over me. Too many things have gone wrong lately—Penn getting banished to Earth, humans popping up on my list before their time, the missing Guardians, and now *this*. I can't help but wonder if all these problems are connected, but if so, the nature of that connection eludes me.

I look back and forth as I listen to the crying. It's very loud, but also a little muffled. I walk to the place where it's loudest, following the noise. There's a symbol carved into the side of the stone wall, and as I get closer, I can make out the outline of a door. Frowning, I can't resist the urge to touch the symbol. It seems oddly familiar, as if I've seen it before, maybe in the handbook given to new Reapers. Three distinct swirls connect in the center, surrounded by a thin circle that joins them all together. What does it mean? Death? It seems cyclical, so maybe death and rebirth? I can't quite put my finger on it.

As I trace the symbol with my finger, the door moves slightly. When I cover the symbol with my hand, the door opens fully. Just as expected, there are souls inside, chained and hunched over. Some are silent; some are crying. There are seven in all.

No more than a handful. It's odd to me because souls are normally kept apart in hell. They aren't given an opportunity to seek comfort or encouragement from one another. It's unheard of for seven to be grouped together.

Before I take two steps inside, a pair of haunting green eyes looks up at me. I reaped this very soul only a few days ago. Penn was banished after he created her and fell in love with her. She doesn't belong here in hell; in fact, I'd left her at the gates of heaven. *Kismet.*

A small sob escapes my lips as I go to her. "What are you doing here?" I ask, but she can't answer me. Tears choke her words. I'm not sure if she's crying out of sorrow for what's befallen her, or if she's simply relieved to see me. I tug uselessly on her shackles as she looks over my shoulder in fear.

I left her at the gates of heaven, so why is she chained up in hell?

My mind is already racing when as a pair of demons walks by the doorway. I freeze. I have no idea what they will do to me if they find me here. I don't even know where we *are*. All I know is demons don't need an excuse to punish someone. Nor do Reapers wander the halls of hell alone.

My pulse pounds in my ears as I hold my breath, waiting for the demons to pass the hidden room. Kismet looks at me with sheer terror in her eyes, and I try to smile encouragingly at her. I give a small nod, hoping she knows I'm here to help.

Once I'm certain the demons are out of earshot, which seems to take an eternity, I whisper, "What is this place?" I look around, assessing the room. Each soul is chained with his or her arms above their heads to the outer walls. But there are several pairs of empty chains, and an entire row of chains down the center of the room. Plenty of room for new additions. Some of the prisoners are worse off than others. In fact, one woman in particular seems as if she's literally fading away. She's becoming opaque. It terrifies me. It means her soul is dying, and once that happens, she will simply cease to exist.

I go to her, and to my horror, I recognize her too. This is Nysa, the very first surprise. I remember collecting her. She was so confused. Her soul knew it wasn't her time. But her name was still there on my list of assignments. Undeniable. Irrefutable. It was painful to take her before her time, but we all hoped she was an anomaly—not a sign of a bigger problem. But more and more surprises popped up, and as I look around the small room, I see they're all in here, every single one.

Another demon walks past, so I crouch down, making myself look small and beneath notice. My time is running thin. Then it hits me. This place we're in is a prison. Something clicks into place in my mind, and I remember where I've seen the symbol on the door before—the cyclical waves churning around, bringing the surprises and the prison around full circle.

"The prison of souls has been opened," I whisper.

TWO

"I will come back for you. I promise," I say to the souls trapped in this terrible room. But before I go, I take Kismet's hand. She looks up at me, tears streaming down her face. I see her glance up at Andrew, her soul mate. Penn created these souls as two halves of a whole. They weren't meant to be sitting in hell, rotting away. They were meant for greatness.

There are answers in this room, ones I'm not prepared to retrieve, and so I'm left with more questions than I had before.

"I promise, Kismet." I say to her. But I don't know if I'm getting through to her. When I hear movement outside again, I decide I can't waste another moment. I need to leave so I can get to work on rescuing them. I can't hope to get seven souls out of hell unnoticed. I need help—and a plan.

It's agony to leave them. But I'm no good to them now. Without knowing how to free them, I might as well be trapped in there myself. I consider asking them more questions, trying to get more information, but the sound of another demon walking by spurs me into action. I need help. The others will know how to attack this problem better than I could on my own. I have to leave them, even if it breaks my heart to do it.

I slip back out of the prison, and then wind my way back to the gate. A few demons walk past me, but they pay me no mind.

I'm a Reaper, after all. I don't spend a lot of time in hell, but it's not unusual for me to be here, especially since the Guardians are off duty for some reason. If one of them stops me, I will demand to know where the Guardians are. Hopefully, I'll manage to keep my cool.

Tears stream freely down my face as I arrive at the gate and make my way back out to the mists. I stand in front of the golden door that leads to my home, but instead of going inside, I sob. I cannot get my mind around what's happened, and why. I consider going straight to God with this information, but then I reconsider. He already knows. I'm sure of it. So the question is—did He mean for *me* to find it? If so, why? What am I to do with this information?

The question spurs me into action, although it doesn't dry my tears. The running does that. The more I think about the souls trapped in there, the faster my feet carry me across the heavens to find the banished Fate.

Penn isn't in my room, but I didn't really expect to find him there. It's dangerous for him to wander the heavens on his own, and I told him so before leaving for my shift.

Banishment doesn't come with second chances. If he's discovered, he really will be eliminated. But I'm not surprised he didn't sit still in my chambers. He had to watch me snatch his beloved from him, long before her time, knowing all the while that it wasn't supposed to happen. He wants answers as much as I do, and he must be anxious to see his sister Fates, despite my warnings against doing so.

I asked him to stay out of the weaving room, at least for now, but it's the obvious place to look for him. He can no more resist the pull of that place than a moth can stay away from an open flame. I've been gone all day, so he's had plenty of opportunity.

And maybe it's not such a bad thing that he got a head start on me. We need information from the tapestry of life—data that only Penn or one of the other Fates can get. When I look at it,

I see a beautifully designed weaving of multi-colored threads—the type of diversity that keeps life on Earth, and in the heavens, interesting. But the bigger picture is all I see. As a Fate, Penn can see each thread as an individual life. What's more, he can actually watch that life play out like a soap opera on a TV. For the Fates, who don't actually travel to Earth, it's a way of keeping in touch with the constantly changing human world.

In my hurry to find him, it doesn't occur to me what this news might do to him. Reality kicks in when the weaving room comes into view. He loved Kismet with all of his heart. They grew close in his time on Earth. To find out that her soul isn't in heaven where it belongs will destroy him.

I stop short at the end of the hall. The door to the weaving room is slightly ajar, but I can't see if anyone is inside from this distance. What in the heavens am I going to tell him? It takes only an instant for the answer to bloom inside of me. The truth. I must tell him the truth. We have to save her—and all the others, for that matter—no matter how much it hurts.

I sprint the rest of the way to the weaving room.

As I burst through the door, I instinctively know he's on the other side. I don't even scan the room for him. I just start talking. "Penn. It's Kismet," I say, bending over, leaning on my knees. That last sprint winded me a little. My blonde hair cascades around my face on either side, effectively creating blinders.

"I found her in the prison of souls! We have to save her," I emphatically say.

He's confused. "The what?"

"The prison of souls," I pant out. "It's not supposed to exist, but someone's opened it. And she's trapped in there, along with Andrew and the other five. Penn. They didn't go to heaven, where I left them. Someone's kidnapped them in the worst possible way."

I take a deep breath and stand up straight. As I do, my eye catches some movement to Penn's right. It's Webber. Of all the people who could be in here with Penn, why does it have to be him? He's the one who took over for Penn after he was banished to Earth. He coveted Penn's job for over a century, so he ran off to God to tattle about Penn's mistake, which led to the Fate's banishment. I know he would give him over without even batting an eye, despite the fact that Penn's punishment for returning would be much more brutal than banishment.

"Webber, I didn't see you there," I say, taking care to guard my tone.

Penn answers before Webber can speak up. "He found me here. We have no choice but to trust him, and him us. As he has so kindly reminded me, I'm fallen and have nothing to lose. I could destroy him just as easily as he could destroy me."

I look back and forth between the two Fates, and I can practically see the anger building between them. I've had enough of their constant competition to see who can go farther, faster, and longer. I approach them, frowning deeply. They back into the stools behind them, sinking down into seated positions as I come closer. The tapestry hangs behind them in all its majesty.

"Listen, you two. I'm about sick of the pissing contest between you. I'm only going to say this once, and I'm not pleased that I have to say it at all. Get over yourselves. This isn't about you. This is about saving lives. Human lives. The lives that we've devoted the entirety of our existence to protect and care for." I clench my fists at my sides. I don't think I've ever been this angry twice in one day. Dempsey's attempt to hit me pushed me over the edge, and that act of hate may very well be fueling my rage. Whatever the reason, this is not the time for sibling rivalry or whatever this twisted situation between them has become.

Penn glances at Webber, who's totally cowed into submission.

"Webber, either come with us or don't, but if I hear that you breathed a word about Penn to anyone at all, Penn won't be the only one you need to fear." I stare at him until he nods. In all honesty, I have no idea what I would do to him, except maybe report him for his tattling. I'm not usually much of a rule breaker… at least, not when the normal rules are guiding our lives. But Webber seems to believe me more than *I* do. He shrinks away from me, avoiding my cold, stern stare.

Disgusted, I say, "Penn, let's go." But as I turn to leave, I spot someone else in the doorway.

Galenia, the Fate who determines how humans die, stands there with her mouth open, tears pooling in her clear blue eyes. As the light from the hallway pours in around her small frame, she looks a little angelic.

"Penn," she breathes.

I halt, knowing this reunion will be emotional for both of them. Galenia and Penn worked side by side for centuries, but after his banishment, they had every reason to expect they'd never see each other again. An Earth year has passed since their last meeting, which translates to just over a week here in the heavens.

A smile tugs at Penn's lips as he whispers her name. "Galenia."

She runs to him, and they hug as if it's the last hug two people will ever experience in the history of the world.

"Well, this is a nice love fest," Webber says, making me bristle yet again.

Galenia ignores him completely, and I am happy to follow her lead. "What are you *doing* here?" she asks as fear clouds her joyful expression. "If they find you—"

He cuts her off. "It's Kismet. She's in trouble. And it's not just her. There are others. Something is happening."

She frowns as she considers his words, and then chances a glance at me. I told Penn's sisters about the mysterious deaths just after he was banished, but none of us could figure out what to do. I brought Penn home in the hopes that he could help, but I neglected to share my plan with the other Fates. I thought it would be safer not to involve them. Now, I know I made a mistake. The sheer joy that fills the room makes me wish Horatia—Penn's other sister—was here too.

"What are *you* doing here at this time of night?" Penn asks her.

"I thought I heard voices."

"From your quarters?" I ask.

"No, I was out walking. I couldn't sleep, and anyway, it's nearly time to start the day. There's a lot of uncertainty around here lately. It's not something a Fate deals with well," she says as she looks at Webber. "As I'm sure you well know."

Webber seems to shrink back into his chair. "I'm sorry," he quietly says. I'm pretty sure Galenia is the only person to whom Webber has ever willingly apologized.

"Horatia will want to help too," she says.

"Too?" Penn asks. "No. I don't want to get you involved. You don't need to endanger yourselves."

"Penn," I say a bit more sternly than I intended. Taking a calming breath, I soften my tone and say, "We need all the help we can get."

He sighs and nods, and it's all the encouragement Galenia needs to bounce joyfully from the room, off to retrieve her sister.

Once she's gone, Penn wastes no time before he starts firing questions at me. "What is the prison of souls, Michaela?"

How can I explain it to him? Somehow, I have to tell him that the human he loves is trapped in hell, her soul withering away in a place that isn't supposed to exist. "The humans refer to it as purgatory—a place where souls would go before their ultimate place in the heavens was decided. The problem was that they could stay there indefinitely. It was unnatural. A soul needs a home, a place, even if it's hell. Plus, those who ran the prison were... unsavory. They tended to go outside their duties to punish the souls inside. So, centuries upon centuries ago, the prison was sealed, although many of the humans still think it exists. To be trapped in there is a fate worse than death."

"Punish?" he asks, his voice thick with uncertainty, and I cringe, upset that he zeroed in on that word.

"Try not to think about it," I say, imploring him to move on.

"So who could have opened it now? Who would even be capable of doing such a thing?" Webber asks timidly from his stool next to Penn's now-empty seat. Once he realizes he's drawn my attention, he returns his gaze to the gold sandals on his feet.

I shrug, attempting to exhale my frustrations in one heavy sigh. "Aside from God, I don't know. And since He was the one who closed it in the first place, I can't see Him reopening it. The demons that run the outer gates of Hell don't have the resources or the intelligence for something like that. Their jobs are simply to keep those who belong inside, and those who don't out. They're the ones I found wandering closest to the prison."

"So, if God is capable of closing the prison, why not take this to Him? I think He could wrap this up in a nice little package for us," Webber persists.

After taking a moment to think about it, Penn offers an answer. "Maybe He's using us to do just that." All I can do is smile and nod. I'm so grateful that Penn is back home to help us make sense of this mess.

"How did you even find it?" Penn asks as he paces around the weaving room.

Knowing his sisters will be back soon, I give him a two-minute synopsis, ending with what I found inside the strange room.

"I'm not sure what's worse. The souls I saw trapped there or the shackles lined up on the walls. There were so many empties." I pause and look at Penn for reassurance. What lies ahead is so… frightening, like nothing we've ever faced in our centuries of predictable routine. "This isn't over, Penn. Not by a long shot," I finally add.

We stare at each other for a long moment, sharing a knowing look, and then I suddenly remember the note I was given by Fia, his mentor, and a former Fate who retired to Earth when Penn took her place. "I almost forgot." I pull out the letter and a small package from a hidden pocket in my dress. "It's from Fia. I really like her."

After I brought him back to the heavens with me, he asked me to deliver a note to Fia to assure her and the rest of his friends back on Earth that he was all right. I stopped in New York to see her before picking up Dempsey. She asked if I could linger a moment or two so she could write a response. Of course, I could hardly say no to that.

As I watch Penn read the note while munching a cookie Fia sent, I reflect on how far he's come in such a short time. Penn's time on Earth has changed him, and so has his love for Kismet. Fates are naturally inflexible, perhaps because they know what the future holds for so many souls, but his time on Earth seems to have taught him there's more to life than just creating it. In spite of our dire circumstances, the thought makes me smile.

Then Horatia, the third Fate, bursts into the room, followed quietly by Galenia. She's different from her sister Fate in almost every way. She exudes confidence as she crosses the room, her dark hair flowing behind her. Her gold robes billow behind her straight, almost rigid form as she grabs Penn in a huge hug. They spin around.

"I thought I'd never see you again," she says through tears. Normally, she maintains a tough exterior. In fact, I don't think I've ever seen her cry. The sight brings tears to my own eyes.

"Me too," is all he can manage.

She clears her throat after Penn puts her down. "So, what's the plan?" She is always ready to spring into action, which is why I love her. We need that now.

"To save Kismet and the others," Penn answers simply.

We stand in a circle, and I know this is the start of something big. I take Penn's hand, and Galenia and Horatia follow suit. Even Webber joins in.

"So now what? We sing *Kumbaya*?" Webber asks.

We all chuckle. I have to believe we will be enough to save this world. These seven souls are a sign of a cancer on Earth, a disease that will kill it if we don't intervene. There is too much good. Too much light. Too much joy to let it fade away, buried inside the prison of souls. No. We will stop it. We will be enough.

THREE

Unfortunately for us, the workday is starting. People are bustling around outside, and I know we can't stand around in the weaving room forever. But we don't have time to come up with a plan of action either. Besides Penn, each of us has responsibilities that can't be ignored during the coming day. Not only would people notice if the three Fates stopped working, but production of human life would come to a screeching halt, and the number of ghosts I would leave in my wake if I took an unplanned day off would be disastrous.

"What should we do?" Horatia asks, searching each of us for answers with her dark chocolate eyes.

"We all have to get back to work. We need to try to stay ahead of whoever's behind these surprises. Penn, I need you to take the lead here, since you aren't working. Find out what you can while we're gone." He nods. "Webber, do what you can to increase your production. We need you to step up, now more than ever," I say, but he glares at me in response.

"Like I haven't been trying hard enough already," he answers, his voice low and thick with hurt.

Sometimes, I feel a little sorry for him, but I'm short on patience today. I shake my head. "Webber, now is not the time for self-pity. We need you to get to work. That's all. Do your best, and I'm sure it will be better than nothing."

Penn claps his hand on Webber's shoulder. "Hey, it'll be fine as long as you don't make an accidental stillborn," he says, making a joke about how he was banished. It's nice of him to try to make Webber feel better, particularly after everything they've been through, but Webber doesn't laugh. He shrugs Penn's hand off and heads into the Fates' workroom, moving just out of earshot.

Horatia leans in and lowers her voice. "He's a bit of an unknown. Think we can trust him?"

Galenia looks sadly after him. "He's not an unknown. He's told us who he is over and over again. It's up to us whether we want to accept that."

I nod. "I agree. But I think we're kind of stuck with him now. He knows too much for us to move forward without him."

Penn frowns, but he doesn't comment further. "I'm the only one who's free today. What should I do? I want to stay here and examine the tapestry, but the new Weaver will be here any minute. I can't linger."

I shift my weight. I have no idea what to tell him. Everything is happening so quickly, and I have no answers.

"We have to go back into hell to get them out of the prison of souls, right?" he asks me.

I nod.

"Okay, then I'm going to spend my day with the Keepers to find out everything I can about what we'll be up against. I'm already dressed like a Keeper, so I shouldn't draw too much attention."

"Yes." I nod emphatically. If anyone in the heavens has the knowledge to help us, it's the Keepers. Their duty is to maintain all the knowledge of history, science, and creation, both on Earth and in the heavens. "That sounds perfect. We can reconvene in my quarters at the end of the day."

We all nod and part ways, but not before I remind Penn to pull up the hood of his Keeper uniform. If he's discovered, we'll probably never see him again—he'll simply disappear. With everything that's going on, it's more than I can bear. My breath hitches in my throat as I watch him cover his blond curls with his hood.

Penn's sisters join Webber in the Fates' workroom. They look miserable, all of them, but we have no choice but to try and proceed as normal, impossible as it feels to concentrate on work with the knowledge that Kismet and the others are waiting desperately for us to help them. But we are the ones who keep the world turning; we are the bringers of life and death. We must do our duty, for now at least.

Penn and I walk together to the common area at the center of heaven. We part ways there. Before he gets too far away, I whisper, "Good luck."

He gives a slight nod and walks on ahead. I hope to God this isn't the last time I'll see him. If he's punished for returning to the heavens, it will be my fault. And even though he won't leave behind a ghost like the human souls who become lost on Earth, I know the knowledge of my failure will always haunt me.

All the Reapers, me included, gather in the naming room each morning. It's a large room lined with huge screens that remarkably resemble the newest black LED TVs on Earth on three of the four walls. Names scroll across the screens, and after the one on top is collected and taken home, another appears at the top. This goes on throughout the day.

We wait anxiously for our assignments, making idle chatter as we do so. I know all the Reapers, and they all know me. But that doesn't mean we're close friends, per se. The Reapers are a solitary group, which is part of what attracts me to the Fates. I see how close they are, and I can't help but want to be a part of that.

A few of us gather around to chat while we wait for the meeting to begin. Though the conversation veers away from any talk of the surprises, it's obvious we're all thinking about it.

"Yesterday, I had a woman try to reason her way out of coming with me," Ariel says with a smile. A tall, thin Reaper, she has beautiful blue eyes and jet-black hair.

"Reason?" I ask.

"She threw science and statistics at me, giving me things she believed to be facts as reasons for staying behind. It wasn't that she didn't believe in the heavens, God, or whatever. It was that she didn't believe it was the right place for her." She makes a clucking sound and shrugs. "In the end, I had to work late last night because of her delays." We all shake our heads with her, commiserating.

"She came with me eventually, but still…"

I nod, feeling her pain. I've been there. The souls who are reluctant to leave Earth can be frustrating.

We go on swapping stories about our silliest humans and the ones who touched us, delaying thinking about the coming day.

Even if there isn't another surprise death, we all know we will have more work to do today than usual. One of our Reapers is on leave. I try not to be too irritated about it, but it really is a terrible time for a vacation. We're in crisis here, and he's off gallivanting who knows where. My last vacation was nearly a century ago. I went to Bora Bora and relaxed. It was gorgeous and lush, but it didn't take long for me to grow lonely—humans can't see me, and I went alone. I wonder if Nathair is lonely wherever he is. Probably not—most of the other Reapers are loners.

I take a deep breath and hold it as the head Reaper takes his position in front of us. He walks up onto the platform along the side wall of the long room and clears his throat. We brace ourselves for another surprise death. Typically, he'll tell us first thing in the morning if an unexpected name has appeared on the list. It's difficult to see individual cuts on the tapestry with so many millions of threads, so our first indication of a problem tends to be when a surprise name pops up. Once we know who it is, the Weaver has no problem finding the damage.

"Good morning, fellow Reapers," Ryker says. His deep voice booms out across the naming room. He has a huge, imposing presence, made even more so by his black-and-white Reaper's uniform. He's not someone I've ever wanted to question.

"Here are your day's assignments." He pauses and waits for us to receive our lists. As always, they just pop into our minds. It's like listening to a radio transmission through headphones, except there is no radio or headphones.

My list is exhaustingly long, but I notice nothing out of the ordinary. I glance at the Reaper next to me, silently searching for any hints at a surprise, but she shrugs her shoulders. Apparently, she didn't get one either.

"Thankfully, there have been no surprises today," Ryker says. "Let's be grateful for that as we move forward with our day. Good luck."

The group mumbles some sort of thanks, and then we separate. No surprises today. That is something to be heartened by as I face my daunting list.

As a group, we file to the golden gate, and Reaper after Reaper disappears into the mists to pursue his or her first soul of the day. I linger for a moment, watching the others vanish until I am left alone in the mists. I glance to my left, thinking about the black gate and how I'm going to sneak the others into hell to help me save the prisoners. An idea tickles at the back of my mind, but it's not something I can focus on at the moment. My list demands my attention. Right now, my world exists for Irene Small.

Irene comes easily. She lived a long and happy life, which is very refreshing for me after the night I had. The rest of my list follows suit. Only a few of the souls resist me, which makes my efficiency outstanding for the day. I even take several names for some others who were having more trouble with their souls. Unfortunately for me, not for them, none of my souls went to the black gate, which is almost unheard of for a day's work. The one day I want to do some reconnaissance in hell, every last soul goes straight to heaven. I suppose if that's the worst of my problems, I'm doing all right, but it's cold comfort.

By the end of the day, I've helped over ten thousand people find their way to their eternal homes. It's exhausting, but there is nothing more fulfilling for a Reaper.

For the first time in over a week, I end my day feeling good. Refreshed. But that changes when Ryker summons us to a meeting. The sound of his voice in my head is clearer than if he were broadcasting the message on a radio. "Reapers, please assemble in the naming room at your earliest convenience." I recognize his tone—it's not to be ignored—so I rush from the mists to find out what's happened.

It's highly unusual for there to be a meeting at the end of the day, and they are rarely used to announce good news. My stomach twists itself into knots as we file back into the naming room to hear what Ryker has to say.

He doesn't speak until we're all gathered before him. "Thank you for coming back," he says. "I know you are all anxious for a break. Today was a wonderfully productive day, thanks to the extra efforts of a few Reapers. When we all come together as a group, it's a beautiful thing," he booms. But I can tell by his stiff posture and stern expression that he didn't just bring us here to thank us.

"But that's not why I've kept you late today. I have some news. Nathair is officially missing." A collective gasp sucks the air from the naming room as we all try to absorb this unexpected news. Nathair is *missing*? How can such a thing even be possible?

I immediately wonder if this is somehow connected to the surprises, and if so, is Nathair the one orchestrating them? I can't imagine a Reaper purposefully cutting lives short, so I decide to give him the benefit of the doubt... for now. But the questions linger.

I'm still struggling to comprehend the news when Ryker continues. "We suspected foul play back when he first disappeared over a week ago, but we wanted to confirm he was indeed missing before announcing it to you. I can assure you that those of us in upper-level management are doing everything we can to find him. I even have a few Archangels on the job. Unfortunately, the only thing we know for sure about his sudden departure is that he isn't on leave. He didn't take vacation. And he hasn't reported his whereabouts to anyone in the heavens."

He pauses and surveys our faces. I glance around to see what he sees. The expressions around me are filled with anger, confusion, and fear. I must say, I'm leaning toward fear myself, but it's not just me.

"Are we in danger?" someone up front shouts out. There's an edge to her voice that makes me turn back to look at Ryker for reassurance.

His face is stony and expressionless as he says, "There's no evidence to point to any of you being in direct danger. Let me repeat that. We do not believe you are in danger. At all. We are not sending you as lambs to the slaughter."

I clear my throat, but someone else beats me to the punch. It's a Reaper behind me. Sophia. She came on shortly after I did, so her seniority should help her stay grounded. Still, the fear in her voice is unmistakable when she asks, "How do you know for sure?"

He pauses a moment before answering, as if searching for an answer that will satisfy us. "I suppose we don't. But the information we have indicates there's no reason for the rest of you to be concerned. For now." The end of his statement makes me wonder. What does he mean *for now*? Is there more danger ahead? Does he believe the missing Reaper is only the beginning of our problems, and if so, doesn't that mean the rest of us *are* in danger? Does the danger stop with us? All signs point to no, that it doesn't, and it's more than a little troubling.

As more and more questions race through my head, I select the one that seems most pressing. "Excuse me, sir. But do you think this is related to the surprise deaths?" I ask, taking care to speak loud enough for him to hear me, but not so loudly that it seems like I'm demanding something. It's a fine line in such a large group.

His expression softens when he sees me, and he sighs. "I don't know, Michaela, but the timing is certainly coincidental. He disappeared right around the time the surprises started popping up. I just don't have enough evidence to make a conclusive link between the two events."

"But you know enough to say we're not in danger?" a loud,

angry voice calls out. "Who's to say another one of us won't end up 'on leave' by the end of our next workday?" The man is two rows in front of me, and I immediately recognize him. Heth is my Webber. I try very hard to get along with everyone, even Webber, but this guy tests my patience. It's as if his only source of joy is to antagonize everyone around him. No one is safe from him, not even our boss.

Ryker stares hard at him, but he doesn't back down. They share a few silent, tense moments, and I have to remind myself to take a deep breath. This is their battle, not mine. "That's right. As I've already explained, you're not in danger," our boss says, as if daring the defiant Reaper to question him further. When he doesn't, Ryker relaxes his jaw slightly and adds some words of encouragement. "I know this is difficult news to take. Never in the history of our existence has one of us gone missing. Believe me when I say we are doing everything we can to not only get to the bottom of this, but also to keep the rest of you safe. Never forget who is in control around here. Try to take comfort in that."

He excuses himself and walks off the small platform. The crowd parts for him as he makes his way to the door. We watch him go in silence, but the moment the door clicks shut behind him, the murmurs turn to rumblings.

It just doesn't add up. Nathair is what I'd like to think of as another gray thread. He's a friend of Heth's, but he keeps to himself, never openly criticizing others or drawing attention to himself. I always figured they were friends because Nathair lets Heth do whatever he wants, and Heth likes that in a companion. The questions return to my mind. What if someone else got to Nathair, and he's just going along with *them*? What if that person is really the cause of the surprises... and Nathair is helping?

"This is an outrage." Someone interrupts my thoughts. "How could they knowingly endanger us this way? We're sitting ducks." I turn to argue the point, but someone else joins the bandwagon.

"I'm not going to work again until this is resolved," a woman says. She's new, and only finished her training last week.

"How can you abandon your post so readily?" I ask. "You haven't even been working with us for that long."

She glares at me. "You want to put yourself in danger, go right ahead. I'm not stopping you. But you don't have authority over me, so excuse me if I don't care what you think of me." She pushes past me on her way out.

I stand there as the rest of the Reapers file out around me, a loud handful of them spouting off phrases like "I won't stand for this" and "the humans aren't worth it." Finally, they're all gone, and I'm alone in the naming room.

My stomach is curdling. I want to throw up, but I also want to rage at them. How can they be so selfish? Reapers are made by God to be compassionate, understanding beings. We're supposed to think of ourselves last. Granted, we've never been in any real danger before, but still… I stand there, staring at the closed glass doors as disgust and rage war inside of me. But I don't have time to dwell on the problem.

I have a date with the Fates.

FOUR

They're all waiting for me in my room when I get there. I spent the short walk back fuming about the irresponsible Reapers threatening to quit. My inner conflict must be playing out on my face because Galenia, Horatia, and Penn all ask, "What's wrong?" in unison. Webber is the only one who doesn't seem to notice my distress.

"One of the Reapers is missing."

"What?" Galenia asks, horrified. "How can that be? What happened?" Her questions are no different from my own, so I just stand there and stare back at her for a moment. Finally, I say, "I don't know. The head Reaper didn't have any answers for us. He just assured us that we're not in any danger."

"How can he know that?" Penn asked.

"He wouldn't knowingly lie to us, so he must truly believe it. But maybe he's just in denial. My instincts are telling me this must be related to the surprise deaths. It's too coincidental."

"Do you think the missing Reaper opened the prison?" Penn asked.

"I…" My mouth hangs open. I don't want to admit it, and it stings to have it out in the open. "Why would one of our own do that?" My mind races at the possibilities. What would he stand to gain from cutting those humans' threads short and then trapping them in that place? Still, the two had to be related, right?

"I don't know," Penn answers, clearly frustrated as he paces around the room. "But it makes sense that a soul from the heavens is involved. How else could they access the prison… or the tapestry, for that matter? Do you think there are larger forces at work here?"

It's not something I want to consider. If faced with the devil himself, I'm not sure the five of us could win. So I ignore the question entirely.

"How could one of us do something so horrible? We all know the humans are important. They're the whole reason we're here. Without the humans, we have no purpose, no need to exist. I just…" Tears choke the rest of my words away.

Galenia puts a hand on my shoulder. "I know. You can't understand how someone among us could do something so evil. I don't either." She rubs my back as the tears stream down my face.

Horatia is the one who breaks the silence. "So what are you going to do, Michaela?"

"What do you mean?" I ask, confused by her question.

"Are you going to keep working?" She says it as if the choice is truly that black and white, without a million variables muddying it up.

"Well, of course. If I quit because I'm scared of something happening to me, think of all the human souls that might be left behind to wander the Earth." I shudder, but I don't let myself dwell on it. "Do you think the others will really refuse to work? Honestly, I assumed it was a lot of talk, and they'd reconsider after having some time to cool down. I don't think any of them will actually go through with it, do you?"

Penn looks at me and wrinkles his chin. "I hope you're right, Michaela."

I shake my head. We have bigger problems at the moment, and I struggle to focus on them. "Well, this is a problem for to-morrow. For now, we have plans to make," I say, forcing a smile. "Did you learn anything useful from the Keepers, Penn?"

Penn nods. "I learned everything I could about hell. It's full of mazes, traps, torture chambers, and things worse than you can imagine. This won't surprise you, Michaela, but our rescue attempt isn't going to be fun at all."

Webber scoffs, earning glares from everyone in the group, even sweet Galenia. I wonder, not for the first time, if it's right for us to force Webber to participate in our plan.

"It seems like there are a few main areas of hell," Penn continues, and I nod, familiar with the levels of hell. "Like all the mazes are in one spot, the torture chambers are somewhere else, and so on. Michaela said the prison of souls is on the outer circle, so with a bit of luck, we can get in and out undetected."

He looks to me to confirm this hope, but I'm not sure I can, so I just shrug. "Demons constantly patrol the outer circle. If we're bringing seven human souls with us, we'll be seen. I can guarantee it."

"So how do you propose we do it?"

"Getting out will be a problem, but I have some thoughts on how we might get in." I hesitate, not sure what they'll think of my plan, but I've been chewing it over since I walked into the mists this morning. I think it might work.

"Let's hear it. If we can get in, maybe we can wing it on the way out," Penn says, taking a one-step-at-a-time approach. I smile at him, appreciating his newfound humanity. Before his banishment, he was very cautious about following the rules. But now he's ready to wing it at a moment's notice, and I love that about him.

"Since we're about to be a little shorthanded, no one would think twice about me training new Reapers." I pause to let that sink in, and then take a look at each of them in turn. "In fact, new Reapers often get tours of heaven and hell, so they can empathize with the souls they help transition. The only thing that would be out of place would be to have more than one trainee with me. However, given the circumstances, I believe I could get the demons to look the other way quite easily."

"I'm not sure I like the idea of trying to hoodwink the demons," Penn says. "But I can't say I have a better plan. After spending some serious time looking things over today, I don't mind telling you all that this feels like a suicide mission. And if we all die, who'll be around to make it right?"

I smile sadly at him. "You've been on Earth too long, my friend. We wouldn't die. We would either spend an eternity in hell or be erased from existence. Our kind does not die." When I hear myself say it, it sounds odd. My voice is so soft and soothing; some call it melodic. To use it to say such dark things feels wrong in every possible way.

Penn walks over and puts a hand on my shoulder, reminding me of our trip back through the mists after Kismet's death. He is a dear friend. I would hate to lose him, particularly as a result of my poor judgment.

"Yes. Thank you, Michaela," he says in a quiet voice. He's not saying it to scold me, or because he's irritated I've reminded them of the risk we're taking. He's simply telling me that we're on the same team. I put my hand on his and squeeze.

"So, what do you think?" I ask the group.

Horatia is the first to speak up. "Go into hell cloak-and-dagger style? I'm in."

Penn nods. Webber looks ill, but to my surprise, he nods too.

"Webber. You're in? I thought for sure you'd want to stay behind," I say.

Swallowing hard, he glances at Galenia. "I mean, I'm in if… everyone else is." I'm not so sure. I can tell he's not fully committed, and we need everyone to be on board one hundred percent. Hell isn't a forgiving place, and once we're in, there's no turning back.

"Webber, no one will judge you if you want to stay behind. In fact, we might *want* someone to stay, just in case we don't come back. You can hold down the fort, explain what happened, and send people after us if need be." I try to sweeten the deal to give him an out.

But his face hardens at the challenge. "I said I'm going." His tone is short. I pushed a button, and I'm not sure which one.

I shrug. "Wonderful," I say, trying to mean it.

Galenia is the only one who hesitates to respond. "I have a bad feeling about this," she says, and I hold my breath. "We can't just go barreling into a place like hell without an exit strategy. Especially if we expect to escape with seven human souls."

Penn turns to me. "Do any of the souls actually belong in hell? If so, it would make our job easier."

"No. They were all taken from the gates of heaven," I answer sadly, wishing I knew how or why.

"I hate to say it, but I agree with Galenia. We need a way to get out," Penn says.

"Okay, well, I came up with our plan of attack. Does anyone else have an idea for a way out?" I say, feeling helpless and derailed.

Penn squeezes my shoulder before walking away and resuming his pacing. "Seven souls."

"Is there any way we could get them out one at a time? Perhaps swap clothes with them or something? Leave one of us behind and come back for him or her later?" he suggests.

"I don't know. Is anyone willing to stay behind in hell?" Horatia asks.

"I will," I offer. Of course I will. I'm the one who found them, and it was my idea to go there in the first place. It seems right for me to stay with the lost souls. I'm a Reaper. Maybe I can offer them some comfort while we wait for rescue.

Galenia smiles sadly at me. "It can't be you, dear Michaela. You're our ticket in— and out—of hell."

I sink down onto the couch behind me. She's right, and it weighs heavily on me, pressing me deeper into the couch cushions. I can't help them. I can't do my duty as a Reaper. It's a strange, almost out-of-body feeling, and I don't like it.

The last time I felt this useless was… well, never actually. I wasn't made specifically to be a Reaper. I was given a choice. I could have been an angel, a Keeper, or a Fate. But reaping is what drew me. The level of compassion the job requires has always come naturally to me. God warned me I wouldn't fully fit in among the Reapers, but I knew that would be true no matter what vocation I chose. Usually, I don't question that I made the right decision, but tonight, I need to accept the fact that I won't be able to do my job the way I'd like.

"I'm happy to do it," Galenia offers. "I'm not imperative to the mission. Maybe I can offer them some comfort."

"Oh, sure, the Fate who spends her days thinking about how many different ways she can kill them is going to be super comforting," Horatia teases. "I'll do it. I'll stay behind."

"To be fair, you're the one who cuts their threads. I just decide how they die," Galenia says evenly.

Penn laughs at them, bickering like a couple of… well, sisters, and it occurs to me again how long these three have worked together. "I'll stay behind. Kismet won't be the first one out. I'd like to stay with her and Andrew."

"Why wouldn't you want your precious Kismet to be the first one out?" Webber asks, a hint of surprise in his voice.

"He's right," I say. "Nysa will have to be the first one out. She's in the worst condition. If we want to save her from extinction, she has to be the first."

"And if whoever brought them there returns while Penn is in her place? Don't you think that person will notice Nysa isn't Penn? They don't really bear a striking resemblance," Horatia wryly says.

"Nysa is black, Horatia. You don't look like her either. Quit trying to take my spot," Penn says.

She pouts, knowing she's been defeated.

"Horatia, I'll need you and Galenia both to help me keep watch for demons. I also might need help coaxing Nysa out. I don't expect her to be terribly aware of her surroundings when we return. She was in rough shape the last time I saw her. She may need… convincing."

"What will we tell a demon if we see one?" Galenia asks, her eyes filled with fear. I can't tell if it's fear of hell or fear for Nysa. Maybe both.

"I think we'll have to tell them that one of the trainees isn't quite cut out for reaping yet. That her weak stomach was deeply affected by the things she saw in hell. Just because it's uncommon doesn't mean it's unheard of," I offer. It's thin, and I know it. The others exchange uncertain glances.

"It might work," I say with a shrug.

"It's the best we have for now. We will have to put this into play tomorrow night," Penn says. We've spent too much time talking to do anything more tonight, especially if we don't want to get caught midway through our mission. "If we come up with anything better in the meantime, we can execute that."

I stretch out on the couch, not sure how to face the upcoming workday, or the night that will follow.

"I'm not sure what to do with myself tomorrow," Penn says, a bit forlorn.

"You could just relax. Get ready for our trek through hell," Horatia says, and then snorts at her own joke.

"I know what you can do to help," I say. "We need extra Reaper uniforms. You're already in this section of the heavens for the day. I was going to grab them on my way back from my shift, but if you're looking for something to do, go for it."

"Michaela, how exactly is a Keeper supposed to acquire Reaper clothes?" he asks.

"Use your imagination. The closet where we keep our uniforms is just by the gate. There isn't too much foot traffic back there once we're all out on assignment. Wait an hour or two after the workday starts, and go for it. You should be fine." I sound more confident than I feel. My plan to take all of my dearest friends into hell has left me shaken and unsure of myself. Why is this a good idea again? Oh, right. Because the fate of humanity rests on getting into that prison, rescuing those inside, and finding out exactly what is going on.

We are reluctant to part ways, even though we have several hours before the workday starts. So we spend our time in my room playing games, laughing, and bickering. To be honest, we're all a bit sad when it comes time to report for our duties.

"Okay, so I'll see you all back here tonight, ready to march into hell," I say, forcing a smile. Their expressions are grim, but they all nod in response.

We part ways silently, each going to our respective workstations, and I turn to look back at the Fates. Horatia and Galenia hold hands while Webber walks in front of them. Penn looks longingly at them, and I know he wants to join them. I notice his fingers are twitching, as if they long to spin the threads of life, but he absently puts his hands behind his back.

Even though I know I'm at risk of being late, I want to comfort him. "There's work to do, Penn. We need to focus."

He nods and smiles, but I can tell it's mostly an attempt to reassure me. "Get to work," he says. Out of nowhere, he slaps me on the butt. I squeal and he laughs, lightening both of our moods.

"That's one for the rumor mill," he calls to me as I hurry away, rubbing my backside. When I brought him back to the heavens, he joked about the rumors that would spread if anyone saw me bringing a Keeper into my room. Heavenly beings don't have illicit affairs. We just don't feel the need for them. And often those who do indulge in a romantic relationship are judged for being too similar to the humans.

Heavenly beings have an irrational fear of ending up like Penn, ruled by their emotions when it comes to life and love. Personally, I don't see what's so bad about that. Penn is unique. Except now, he's just drawn more attention to himself at a time when he's supposed to do the very opposite. I glance around as I'm walking away, but by sheer dumb luck, no one is around to have witnessed my spanking.

I shake my head, thinking of how much I've missed Penn, hoping this workday goes by quickly so we can dive into our real work. In hell.

FIVE

I feel hopeful as I walk to the naming room to get my assignments for the day. Maybe the other Reapers will have settled down after a night of rest and relaxation. Maybe they'll be less angry and more helpful. Maybe.

But as I weave my way into the group of my fellow Reapers, nodding polite greetings as I go, I can tell my hope is in vain. Everyone is tense, and the mumbling is loud enough to create a faint rumble throughout the room. A hush falls over the space as the head Reaper takes his position on the platform. He's such a huge presence up there; I can't imagine defying him. But I feel like some of my colleagues are about to try. I cringe as he opens his mouth.

"All right, thankfully, there are no surprises to announce today. There's also no news about Nathair. I'm sorry. As soon as I know something, I will pass it along to you. Currently, we are trying to pinpoint his last assignment, which will help guide our work. You all have a fair amount of freedom to go where you please in your downtime, so he could be anywhere."

He isn't wrong. Some Reapers choose to spend their downtime in exotic locations on Earth. Humans can't see us unless it's their time, so we can go anywhere. I've seen some lovely things on Earth. Waterfalls, glaciers, rolling hills, mountain ranges, tropical islands. The ancient buildings and ruins of Europe have their own special charms, reminding me of reapings gone past. Traveling the world is a wonderful way to decompress and re-center.

But from what Ryker's said, it sounds like Nathair wasn't actually approved for vacation. He really could be anywhere. I sigh, trying to stave off the hopeless feeling weighing me down. I only need to get through the day.

As our assignments start filtering into our minds, the boss keeps talking. "Here are your assignments for the day. As always, I hope you all have a good and productive day."

But as he was signing off, a few of the Reapers walked over to a cluster of tables and chairs along the opposite wall of the naming room and sat down. A few others followed, until a group of six is gathered around the tables.

"I will not be working under these conditions," Heth says. Of course he's their leader.

"Nor will I," the others say, one right after the other, until all the dissenters have voiced their grievances.

No, I think. This isn't happening. It's not in our nature. Although reaping isn't normally a dangerous job, we're simply not built to think of our own well-being first. The humans are our priority. But wishing the problem away is like trying to hold back the ocean with my bare hands.

Ryker's eyes turn cold and hard. I shrink back from his huge presence and brace myself for what's coming. I expect him to yell, to force them to work, to punish them, to threaten them, to do *something*. But he doesn't. Instead, he stops halfway down the platform and looks down at all of us.

"Your actions do not come without consequence. Remember that." His voice is low and menacing. I have no idea what he means by that, whether he's talking about the huge influx of ghosts Earth is bound to see after today's work, or if there will be an actual punishment for the dissenters. He doesn't elaborate. But after seeing what happened to Penn for his single spinning mistake, I know justice is swift and harsh here in the heavens. I shudder to think what will happen to them.

"Those who remain will each be given extra names to account for… our losses. Thank you." He looks directly at me and I nod, then he exchanges looks with a few of the others who are still standing in front of the platform. Without saying anything more, he turns to leave. We watch him silently, our group now divided between working Reapers and dissenters.

After he's gone, and the Reapers are starting to scatter—at least those of us who are still willing to work—I climb up onto the platform and walk behind Ryker's podium. I have no idea what's gotten into me, but I have to say something. I have to try to make them understand who they're hurting. I know I'll regret it if I don't make an effort.

"Guys, what are you doing? Don't you understand how many people will be left behind because of your selfish choices? The humans are the reason for our existence. Our purpose is to care for them. To make sure they get safely to their eternal homes. If you turn your back on that, what will you be? If you are not a Reaper, who are you?" I'm panting by the end of the speech. The stresses of the week are catching up to me, and something that feels like what the humans describe as an adrenaline rush is washing over me. Energized by my anger, I clench my fists at my sides.

"Well, aren't you a softhearted one?" Heth says. "Michaela, unfortunately, I couldn't care less what happens to the humans today. I'm more interested in making sure *I* live another day."

"Perhaps I'm not being clear," I snap back. "Think of the child who will be left behind because of your selfishness. Have you ever left a child behind? I did once. It was horrible. The child just wanted to stay with her mother. And she ended up torturing the poor woman for the rest of her life. When I had to take her mother in the end, it was even worse. Now that child wanders the Earth alone." I shudder at the memory. "If you take this path, there will be thousands of children left behind. Not to mention adults. The Earth will quickly be overrun with restless spirits. The Earth is a sanctuary for the humans, and for us, if you really think about that. And it will be ruined. Because of you." I look hard at their faces. A few are unsure. So I strike while the iron is hot.

"It doesn't have to be this way. There's a terribly simple solution. You could come to work. Bring them home."

One of the Reapers speaks up. She's a shy girl who's been working about half as long as I have. She's not very social, so her fearfulness is one of the only concrete things I know about her. I'm not surprised she's standing with Heth.

"But what difference can *I* make?" Her voice is small and quiet, an exact reflection of her.

I smile and climb down from the platform. Taking her hands in mine, I look into her eyes. "Even if you only take one soul home today, you will have made all the difference in *their* world. You will have saved that soul from a terrible, lonely existence. One that can't be reversed." I smile encouragingly at her, and it's enough. She nods her acceptance. One other Reaper joins our group, but there are still four on the selfish side. That means that over forty thousand people could be left behind by the end of the workday if the rest of us can't pick up the slack. I try to focus on my success, not my failure, and I profusely thank the two who have agreed to work. Even if we can't save everyone, we can do a lot.

As we approach the gate leading out to the mists, I work hard to clear my head and concentrate. I need to think about the people I can help. If I don't, they will suffer too, and even more people will be fated to linger on Earth as ghosts. I can't give in to the panic I'm feeling, but this problem seems much more immediate than our trapped souls in hell. *One thing at a time*, I think.

Taking a deep breath, I step out into the mists to collect my first assignment.

Of course, things don't quite go the way I hoped. The dead are slow minded all day long. It's as if they're extra reluctant to come with us because they know something is off. I barely manage to finish my own list, and there's no time to help anyone else.

Everyone else had the same problem, and a few didn't even finish their lists.

All of us returned in defeat at the end of the day. Ryker calls us into the naming room for another meeting, and I worry it's going to be an unpleasant surprise. The anxiety from the day threatens to boil over, and tears build in the backs of my eyes as I wait to hear what he has to say. After all the people we left behind today, I'm not sure I can take more bad news.

Ryker clears his throat as he makes his way to his usual position on the platform. The dissenters sit in the back of the room while the rest of us stand up near the podium.

He doesn't waste time with a greeting or any other formalities. "As you can see, every Reaper who went out today returned home safely." He looks toward the dissenters, who are laughing and joking together. Did they just sit in the naming room goofing off all day while human souls were left wandering untethered? I frown as I watch them throwing a paper ball to each other.

A frown creases Ryker's forehead. "As a result of your… malcontent," he says, staring at them, "9,752 human souls were left behind. Because of you." I follow his gaze, expecting to see a bunch of apologetic, cowed Reapers, but they don't even look at him. Although they've stopped causing a commotion, they still don't acknowledge him. They're busy studying their nails, talking to each other, or fiddling with various belongings.

"I would like to remind each and every one of you that your actions, whatever they are, will have consequences." He returns his attention to those of us who are still gathered around the platform. "Thank you to those who did their best today. You kept the number of souls left behind as low as possible. I hope we can do even better tomorrow, and that more of you will decide to return to your posts." He doesn't sign off; he simply walks off the platform and leaves.

I think I hear the group of dissenters mocking him as he leaves, and I actually find myself worried about them. How could these heavenly beings have wandered so far astray? What will happen to them as a result of their choices? Penn was punished for accidentally cutting one life short, so I know the punishment for their far graver crime won't be pretty. As I pass by,

Heth calls out to me.

"Hey Goody Two-shoes. Seems like your best efforts weren't enough. Why even bother?" he asks, and the others around him laugh. The Reaper next to him claps him on the back.

But I don't have to answer. Miette, the shy Reaper who faced her fears this morning, stands up to them. "Because even one life makes all the difference in the world. It matters." In that moment, I am so proud of her, of what we do, that it doesn't matter what they say in reply. She takes my hand, and we walk out of the naming room together.

"Thank you." I say to her once we're outside the glass doors.

"No, thank you. I nearly made a very bad mistake today. You saved me from it." There's a twinkle in her deep brown eyes as she smiles up at me. Then she retreats, heading toward the quarters hall. I can't help but smile in spite of the dismal day. I made a difference on Earth and in this Reaper's life. Now, if only I can make a difference in hell.

SIX

When I return to my own room, everyone is there waiting for me. They're already dressed and ready to go. Penn is striking as a Reaper, and the uniform fits his sculpted body as if it were made for him. But I'm concerned. Without his Keeper's hood, his face is totally exposed.

"You can't wear that here. You'll be recognized." I think of how unsavory my comrades have been acting and shake my head. "You can't be seen around here. To make matters worse, my peers can't be trusted right now."

"What happened today, Michaela?" he asked.

"Well, there weren't any surprises, if that's what you're worried about."

"That's good?" He says it almost like a question.

"The Reapers didn't change their minds. Four of them stayed behind today, so we left behind almost ten thousand souls. Ten thousand new ghosts who will be doomed to wander the Earth forever. All in one day. It usually takes centuries to create that many ghosts. In fact, there might not even have *been* that many ghosts before today. We might have more than doubled the ghost population on Earth in one day."

Flopping down onto the empty couch, I throw my arm over my eyes, trying to block out that terrible number and the mission that lies ahead. Just when I thought things couldn't get any worse, thousands of souls lost their tickets home, and there's nothing I can do to help them or prevent it from happening again. I'm overwhelmed, so I stop thinking about it. Right now, all that exists is this couch, the darkness behind my eyes, and the sound of my breathing. In. Out. In. Out.

Penn is the one who breaks through my haze. "Michaela, this isn't your fault. I'm sure you did everything you could to save as many people as possible. You can't control other people's choices." He pulls my arm off my face, and I look up at him with shining eyes.

"What you can control is how you react. So tuck in your bottom lip and lead us the hell into hell." He's trying a little too hard, but I appreciate that he *is* trying. I give a token chuckle and swipe at my tears. Galenia is watching me as I sit up, and I can almost see her broken heart through her clear blue eyes. She tucks her long, brown hair behind her ears, comes over, and silently embraces me. The others say nothing; they simply allow me this moment to grieve for those I lost today. Those *we* lost today. Although it solves nothing, it's exactly what I need.

Eventually, I take a breath. When I look up, Penn is donning his Keeper's uniform and the others are wearing their Reaper outfits.

"Not sure I want to be associated with a Keeper," Webber says, nodding to Penn's clothing. His tone hints at the bit of truth behind his joke.

"We do make a misfit bunch, don't we?" Horatia asks, eyeing herself in her Reaper's uniform. It hugs her body in all the right places, and her dark hair flows down her back, complementing the look quite nicely.

No one answers her, and we look at each other for a moment, each of us undoubtedly thinking the same thing—we are about to go on a suicide mission. But none of us tries to leave or back out. After a few heartbeats, Penn moves to the door and exits. The rest of our group follows, and I bring up the rear.

We walk in silence to the gate in the mists. Penn knows the way by now, so he walks up ahead with his head bowed down.

I glance around as we walk. Horatia's right. We *do* look like a bunch of misfits. I can only hope we don't draw too much attention to ourselves as we make our way toward the gate. Lucky for us, most of the Reapers have adjourned to the common room or their own quarters. Even the dissenters have dispersed, and I find myself wondering if they've already been punished. I still don't quite know how I feel about that. They deserve their fate. But I've worked with many of them for a very long time. The thought of their demise saddens me.

A thought occurs to me as we make our way to the gates of heaven. Maybe they'll be banished to Earth and assigned to manage the ghosts. It's a perfect and appropriate solution. So much so, it makes me smile a little. I consider suggesting it to Ryker, but he has enough on his plate without me trying to tell him how to do his job. Besides, there's no time for stalling.

We make it to the gate without being stopped. Penn goes through first without hesitation. Horatia and Galenia stop abruptly, and Webber nearly collides with them.

"What's the hold up, ladies?"

"We've never been outside before. Ever," Galenia says as she stares at the gate, almost in awe of the golden figures carved on its surface.

Horatia's hand is suspended midair, reaching out for the door but not quite touching it, marveling at it just like Galenia is doing.

"Penn is just on the other side, waiting for you," I say. "This will be an adventure you can take together. Just like old times."

"That makes *me* feel great," Webber flatly says.

"Webber, we all have our own roles to play in this," I say. "Roles that do not require whining."

I nod toward the gate, urging the girls to go through. They look at each other, take a deep breath, and do just that. Webber and I follow before the gate has a chance to close.

"What took you so long?" Penn asks.

I shrug at Penn, handing him his Reaper's clothes, and nod toward the girls, who are walking around the misty area with their mouths hanging open. The three gates are clustered around us in all their glory. Our gate stands behind us, the gate of heaven is to our right, and the gate of hell is to our left. Naturally, everyone is drawn to heaven's gate. They all wander toward it, taking in its beauty. I stand back, allowing them this moment to appreciate one last good thing before we enter a place where the word "good" doesn't exist.

Finally, they turn toward the gates of hell. Webber and the girls shrink away. It's huge, black, and terrifying to be sure. Even Penn, who's already seen it, takes a step back.

"Everyone still on board with our plan?" I ask, unsure of how to proceed. I hadn't anticipated losing them so early in the journey. The things they might see behind the barricades are much worse than the gates themselves. If they can't steel themselves now, they'll never make it back out unscathed.

Galenia is the first to set her jaw and walk toward me, stretching out her hand and pushing through the gate. "Let's go," she says. Horatia follows, then Penn, who's back in his Reaper disguise. Webber falls in behind them, and I bring up the rear, which fits with our cover story. We are a group of Reapers touring hell. Nothing more, nothing less.

Once on the other side, the group lets out a collective gasp. It's certainly an unforgettable sight. Despite the expanse of the cavern we've just entered, it's claustrophobic. The darkness is only eased by the eerie red glow coming from the torches lining the stone walls, and the smell of sulfur permeates the air. I hate crossing into hell. The immediate urge to get out always overwhelms me. Today is no different. My body clamors to turn back, but I stand up straight, taking step after step away from the gate.

"This way," I say, pushing through the group to lead. "Penn, stay at the back to make sure no one lags behind."

He nods and takes his place while Webber walks between Horatia and Galenia. With any luck, we'll pass by undetected. The Reapers aren't working right now, which means the demons aren't either. They're not expecting anyone. They might all be… well, doing whatever demons do in their down time. My heart hopes, but my mind doesn't believe it for a second.

We follow the winding corridors for quite some time, getting so close to the prison that I can hear the moans coming from inside. I glance back at Penn, who has a stricken look on his face.

When I turn back around, I find myself face to face with a demon. His scorched black body hulks over me. The cracks in his skin glow red, matching his eyes, and his black wings extend out on either side of him.

"What are you doing here, Reaper?" he asks, not backing down. Straightening, I look right at him. I can hear the others nervously shifting their weight behind me. I swear one of them is whimpering, and I'm willing to bet it isn't one of the girls.

"We're conducting a tour for new trainees now that the workday is over. Seeing as we're shorthanded, there's no other time for it," I say, trying to sound confident.

He glances over my shoulder. "Quite a large group for this time of night. That one there doesn't seem suited for the job." He nods toward Webber.

I eye Webber, silently urging him to keep his cool. "We need all the help we can get."

"Things must be desperate indeed if you're using the likes of this one."

"Hey," Webber says, clearly feeling wounded. "No one talks to me like that, especially not a lowlife like you."

I tense. It's not a good idea to engage the demons. I glance at Penn, but he's busy glaring at Webber.

"Lowlife, hmm? I think you'll find our working relationship requires a bit more respect than that, Reaper." He turns back to me. "He has a lot to learn. You have your work cut out for you," he says. He isn't wrong.

"Well, I'll let you get back to it then," I say, hoping to cut our interaction short.

"I'm not busy. Would you like a private tour? I can show you where we put those who think they are better than others." The malice in his voice makes my skin crawl.

I clear my throat. "No, but thank you. I'm sure you would like to enjoy your downtime. Things have been busy lately."

"How thoughtful of you. But I truly don't mind. There's someone I want to check on anyway. Come. Follow me."

We exchange nervous glances, but ultimately, there is nothing we can do. We have no choice but to follow him. All of us manage to sneak a glare at Webber, who maintains his stiff posture and avoids eye contact with everyone. He doesn't think he's done anything wrong. I sigh, hoping we don't regret the decision to include him.

Much to my chagrin, two other demons join our tour guide at his invitation. They're enjoying this, if for no other reason than to make the new recruits uncomfortable. Trial by fire. Normally, new Reapers handle their first visit to hell relatively well. It can be overwhelming to see all these terrors in one place, but Reapers only come here after receiving extensive training on what to expect, so it's not as much of an assault on the senses as my poor Fates are experiencing.

We walk away from the prison, and I glance over my shoulder at it, catching Penn's eye in the process. His face is red, and while the demon's back is to us, I mime for him to take a deep breath. We're not out of the woods by a long shot, and I need him to stay with me.

I'm not quite sure how we will shake the demons, but I know it won't help if one of us disappears or goes rogue.

After a few twists and turns through the dark caverns of hell, we arrive at an area I've never seen before. There are so many doors on either side of the eerie hallway that I lose count.

"Why aren't these hallways smoky? There are so many lit torches. Seems like we should be choking by now," Horatia asks. I can tell she's trying to focus on anything besides the fact that we're off course and surrounded by demons.

"An observant one," the demon says. It's supposed to be praise, but nothing from his voice would sound positive. Judging from the look on Horatia's face, I gather she feels the same way. "It's not real fire. Only light. You can touch the flames if you'd like." He nods toward the torch nearest us, but Horatia shakes her head no.

"I believe you."

The demon laughs, his colleagues joining in, and the horrible shrieking sound makes all of us shrink back. I fight hard not to cover my ears.

"That would be your first mistake, dear Reaper. Never trust a demon."

"Noted," she says, eying him. He just continues to chuckle as he walks along.

After what feels like an eternity, the three demons stop in a seemingly random spot. The door we stand in front of is black, much like the gate, except there are no intricate designs on it. It's simply a black door that fits perfectly into the rounded archway in which it hangs. The handle feels like a black hole that will suck in the soul of whoever touches it, and I find myself recoiling from it a bit.

The demon opens the ancient door without a second thought. It creaks with age, as if complaining about its sudden use. All I can see inside is blackness. No windows or torches offer any kind of relief.

The demon that originally found us gestures inside. "This is where we keep souls to await processing while we find the perfect home for them here in hell."

"There's no light in there." It flows out of my mouth as a statement, not a question.

"No, there isn't," the demon said, sounding unduly proud. "There's also nothing in there that can hurt them, but they don't know that. The human mind is sometimes all the torture we need around here." His smile is gruesome.

"Perhaps you'd like to see inside." His confident tone makes me hesitate.

But Webber is so puffed up after his perceived slight that he pushes past our group and into the room.

"It's not so scary in here. Maybe you should up your game, demon," he says, goading the demon on.

"Maybe I should," he says as he slams the black door home.

I hear Webber laugh nervously on the other side, and we all uneasily shift our weight.

"Okay, your point is made. Let him out, and we'll just go.

Clearly, this isn't a good time for a tour," I say, keeping my tone as professional and even as possible.

The demon laughs, but this time, there's no glee in it like there was before. He's mocking me.

At the sound of his laughter, Webber starts to panic. Banging on the door, he starts screaming. "Let me out! I am a heavenly being. You *can't* do this to me."

This spurs even more laughter from the demons. "Looks like we just did."

I touch the demon's arm and pull him aside. He looks at my hand, clearly surprised by my action. Contact between us isn't typically physical, but I'm hoping to break him out of this cycle.

He looks at me with eyes that burn with curiosity. "This is enough," I say. "Your point is made. It's time to end this game."

He smiles broadly at me, showing me his gruesome rows of sharp, yellowing teeth, spaced far enough apart to reveal a red glow behind them.

"That's where you're wrong, Reaper. Here in hell, you don't make the rules. I do." He turns to his comrades. "What do you think, boys? A day or two in there ought to teach him some respect."

"You can't do this," I say, my voice rising in panic, but I try to make it sound like anger and authority.

"I already have, dear Reaper. I don't believe you would have been able to teach him the lessons he needs to learn. Come back in a day or two, and maybe we'll let him go."

"That's a lie, and you know it," I say accusingly.

"You're catching on," he says with a grin. He looks at the others, who've remained silent during our exchange. "Seems like your trainees have lost their stomach for the tour. Perhaps I should lead you out."

"I'm not leaving without him." I point aggressively toward the closed door.

Webber continues to scream, but his words have become jumbled by panic, so I can no longer understand what he's saying.

The demon laughs and gestures toward the door. "He didn't

think it was that scary in there. I'd hate to see him in a real torture chamber." His eyes light up as he looks at his companions. "Wouldn't it be a shame if we hid him deeper in hell before you came to retrieve him?" The laughter from the three demons is low and slow. Menacing.

"You *can't* do this. I will report you."

"I don't answer to your authorities, Reaper. And I think my own boss will be quite entertained by my quarry," he answers. "Now, I can escort you out peacefully, or you can join your friend in the empty rooms around him."

"Don't leave me in here!" Webber shouts, finally intelligible.

"I'm sorry," I whisper to him, for it's all the volume my voice will allow. Fear, shame, and anger have taken the life out of it. To the demon, I manage to choke out, "Thank you, sir. I would appreciate an escort out."

"It would be my pleasure," the demon says with a cruel smile. He won, and he loves it.

"Of course. I'm so glad I crossed paths with you," I say. After that, our trek back to the gate is silent, although I notice the longing look Penn gives to the corridor leading to the prison of souls. We're all cowed into submission after what was done to Webber.

When we get to the outskirts of hell, the demon stops walking. "You can take it from here, Reaper. The gate is just there." He gestures behind him. "If you'd like, come back tomorrow night and see if you can find your wayward Reaper. Maybe I'll feel generous and return him to you. But don't get your hopes up. I think we're going to have fun with him."

"I know better than to hope in a place like this, demon," I say, narrowing my eyes at him.

He smiles broadly at me. "Good. I look forward to seeing you again, Reaper." He walks away, leaving us alone in front of the gate.

There aren't any demons milling about this close to the outskirts, so we all stand where we are, looking at the gate in front of us without seeing it.

"Are we really leaving without Webber?" Galenia asks. The

horror in her voice cuts me straight to my core. I fight the urge to crumple into a heap on the floor of hell.

"Of course we are," Penn says. The anger in his voice startles me out of my doom spiral. "His attitude finally caught up with him. He made his own fate, now let him stew in it. I think we should make our way to the prison now that we're alone."

Galenia shakes her head. "He's still our brother. We can't just leave him there."

It's too late. We've spent too much time with the demons. "I'm afraid we have to," I say as a tear winds its way down my face. "For now."

SEVEN

None of us *want* to leave. It's something I never imagined would happen. Hell is such a horrible place that no one would ever choose to stay there, but I just can't bring myself to take that first step outside, knowing we're one man short. If we leave, it's like making it real. Final.

Penn is the first to go out, clearly not as disturbed by Webber's situation as the rest of us. I don't want to leave the girls in hell, but I also don't want to leave Penn wandering around in the mists. As a heavenly being who was banished, he's in almost as much danger out there as he was in hell. I give them each a gentle push, and they reluctantly exit.

I'm the last to go. With one last glance over my shoulder, I whisper to the darkness, "I *will* come back for you." But I know the sentiment will die on my lips without ever reaching Webber's ears. Hell does that to hope.

When I join the others, I see Penn pacing around at the edge of the mists. "Couldn't he watch his mouth for just a few hours?" he demands. "It's his fault that we couldn't get into the prison, not to mention the fact that we were forced to leave him behind."

"It was a mistake to bring him. I should've insisted he stay behind," I say. I shiver as I think about how Webber might be doomed to share my past assignments' fates.

"All he did was make more work for us. Just because he couldn't control his pride in a place that eats that kind of thing up."

"You're right. Hell thrives on those attitudes. Yet another reason why it was a mistake to bring him," I say, starting to wallow in my poor decisions.

"Michaela, stop. You aren't responsible for Webber's actions. He is. When God sentenced me to banishment, I blamed no one but myself for my fate. The punishment was just, so I accepted it. Like on Earth, there are direct consequences for your actions here in the heavens. And Webber is justly feeling his."

"Those are harsh words, Penn," Galenia says.

"That doesn't make them untrue," he says, staunchly standing by his anger.

Horatia goes to him. "You're just angry. Maybe you'll see it differently once you settle down. He was just scared and desperate."

"Would you still feel that way if the demon had taken me instead?" He looks deep into her brown eyes. His question makes me shiver. Would I have given Webber the benefit of the doubt if he were here in Penn's place, and Penn was gone forever?

"No," Horatia says honestly. "But you wouldn't have mouthed off to a demon. So you would never be in that position in the first place."

"Exactly," Penn says. "Webber had full control over his actions. The demon's decision was a direct result of that. And now, instead of helping us, we have one more name on our ever-growing list of souls to save from a horrible existence." His fists clench and unclench, like he needs something to throw.

I sigh heavily as we stand at the edge of the mists. The black gate still looms behind us, but our golden entrance home calls to me.

"The bottom line here is that it isn't our job to pass judgment on Webber," I say. "Our bias comes into play too much, as you have so acutely pointed out. No, I wouldn't feel the same way if you were in his place. But we're not God; we're ill-equipped to sentence him to anything." My voice is swallowed by the mists, leaving us in silence for a time. Penn looks away from me, and his posture slouches a little. I can tell my words reached him, but perhaps they didn't get all the way through. I shake my head, knowing it doesn't really matter.

"I can't believe we had to leave him there though," Galenia says. "What are we going to do?"

"Do you think we should tell God what happened?" Horatia asks.

I laugh, but I don't mean to. It just a release of pent-up energy. "I'm sure He already knows. But I'll bet He'll wait to see how we handle this before intervening."

"So, how do we… handle it?" Galenia asks.

Despite the fact that I've been moving through a fog of disbelief over what happened, my mind has been working hard to think of solutions to our most imminent problems. "I suggest Penn disguises himself as Webber. I know you've been itching to spin anyway, Penn. Just watch your productivity. Webber is slow. If you suddenly have a great day, you'll draw attention to yourself."

"But think of the ground we could make up, Michaela. Our team, back together again." He smiles at the girls and reaches for their hands. They take his gratefully. Standing there in a triangle, they leave me on the outside. The image fills me with mixed emotions; I'm happy to see them back together, where they belong, but I long to be inside that triangle with them.

"I know you'll do what you think is right… and nothing I say will sway you from that path. But please *try* to blend in. You're in more danger now than ever. And for heaven's sake, stay away from the new Weaver. He would be the first to notice. Have Galenia or Horatia deliver all the threads, and make sure to work with the door closed. Be careful."

He nods, as if he knows the risks and willingly accepts them. "It's only a day, Michaela. Anyone can have a good day. Tomorrow night we'll go get him, and he can get back to work."

My laughter sounds bitter. "Right… Assuming the demons let him go, he's totally unaffected by his jaunt through hell, and our decision to leave him there to be tortured doesn't affect his productivity." The pessimism I feel is uncharacteristic, but I've reached my limit of failures for the day.

I know Webber is on his way out anyway, but if this experience does damage his productivity further before a replacement can be found, it will have a vast effect on Earth. Combined with the added ghosts and the surprises, it makes me feel like we're in the middle of a perfect storm.

"He did this to himself as far as I'm concerned," Penn says, his tone dark.

"And as far as I'm concerned, it was my half-baked idea that got us into this mess in the first place. It's as much my fault as it is his." Frankly, I'm hurt by what's happened, even more so by my role in it, and Penn's intolerant attitude is wearying.

Penn breaks the triangle and comes toward me. I turn my back to him, not wanting him to see my pain. But he takes my hand anyway, walking around to face me.

"This is *not* your fault. Maybe the person at fault for this whole mess is the same one who cut those threads short. I don't know." He hesitates and looks over my shoulder at the girls before returning his attention to me. "But I do know one thing. This is dumb. All of this. It's beyond stupid. I shouldn't have fallen in love with a human. I shouldn't have made a mistake bad enough to get banished. People shouldn't be dying before their time. The Reapers shouldn't be letting the humans become ghosts. We shouldn't have gone into hell. And Webber shouldn't still be there. Nothing like this has ever happened, and somehow, we're the lucky crew who gets to deal with half a dozen problems at once? It's all just bat-shit stupid."

I laugh. It's one of those moments where if I don't laugh, I'll cry.

Horatia pipes up. "Dumber-than-a-doornail stupid."

I laugh harder.

"Get-your-tongue-frozen-to-a-lamppost stupid," Galenia offers. "I've seen that happen to humans. It's a real thing," she earnestly adds.

"A-Fate-without-a-fate stupid," Penn says quietly as he

holds both of my hands in his and looks into my face. "But we have each other, and we will muddle through it as best as we can." He looks over at Galenia.

"We're not leaving him in there," he adds to reassure her. "We will go back for him at our first opportunity. Hopefully tonight. I won't even entertain the idea that the demons won't give him up. We're getting him back. Just not right this second. We all have a job to do today, and if we don't work, the problems we're facing will only become worse." The conviction in his voice gives me faith.

I nod. Together, we walk back to the golden door, short one Fate. Despite the fact that our mission was a complete failure, we cling to the hope that it's not over until we quit. And we're not quitting.

———————

Penn changes back into his Keeper's robes before we go through the gate. We stop by my quarters so the three Fates can change back into their robes before heading to work for the day. I urge Penn to stay in his Keeper's robes until he gets to the workshop.

"If you don't, the guards at the weaving room will recognize you, and they'll act first and ask questions later." Archangels had been posted there not long after Kismet was taken in an attempt to stop the damage to the tapestry.

He reluctantly agrees, but I can tell he's itching to wear Webber's spinning robe. I think he just feels good about returning to familiar territory, to the work he loves, and he wants to do it on his own terms. But if he doesn't keep himself hidden, he'll disappear, and he will become one more loss. One more sacrifice to the storm. I'm not sure I could handle that.

We've spent an entire exhausting night in hell, and I'm having trouble facing the day to come. The others don't speak as we go through the motions of getting ready, but I can tell they're just as drained as I am.

I watch them as they head toward the common area on their way back to their workroom, hoping they can get through the day without being caught. I don't believe for a second God doesn't know what we're doing, but if someone forces His hand, He'll follow through with the consequences he laid out for Penn. My friend may be the greatest Fate the heavens have ever known, but he isn't above the rules. He must remain inconspicuous today.

Realistically, no one visits the Fates. There's no need. The Weaver is the only one who sees them at work, and if one of the girls delivers the threads, Penn will be perfectly safe. But the odds haven't been in our favor recently, so I can't help but fret.

My heart is heavy with the things that have happened, and the things to come as I walk to the naming room. How in the heavens am I going to get through the workday, knowing what Webber is going through today? Knowing how many more ghosts will be made today if the strike continues? Knowing how much worse it will be if another surprise is named? Knowing the loss we will all feel if Penn is discovered?

As I take a deep, shuddering breath, Miette appears at my side. She takes my hand and squeezes it.

"Ready?" she asks me with a meek smile.

"Not really," I admit.

"Me neither." But we walk through the glass doors and into the naming room together.

Much to my disappointment, the dissenters still refuse to work. Ryker says nothing. He simply comes in, makes sure we all get our assignments, and leaves. He usually says at least a few words to us—have a good day, good luck, *something*. I've never seen him this silent before, but at least there are no new surprises. It's been a few days since the last one landed. But I don't allow this change to comfort me. Perhaps it only means we're in the eye of the storm, and the worst is yet to come.

I turn to Miette. "Do you think it's over? The surprises?"

"I don't want to let myself hope that's true," she says as we leave. The dissenters are cackling at us the whole way to the door.

When we reach the gate, I wish Miette good luck before we step into the mists. I hope this will be over soon. I'm not sure how much more I can take.

My first assignment is a middle-aged woman who was in the wrong place at the wrong time. Even after all this time, it's hard for me to watch things like this unfold. I still have an instinct to call out, to stop her from turning her car in front of the driver who's looking down at a phone. She dies instantly after her car is hit broadside at forty-five miles an hour. Her soul stays standing where the impact occurred, although her car is clear across the street, sandwiched between a cement light pole and the car that hit her. Emergency vehicles have not yet arrived, and an eerie silence hangs in the air in the moment before people get out of their cars and rush to her aid.

She's looking around rather frantically as I make my approach. I simply reach out my hand, saying nothing. As she looks at me, I smile. She half smiles back, more out of courtesy than genuine intent, before looking back at the wreckage of her car.

"I'm dead, aren't I?" she asks as she brushes at a stray piece of her red hair. She's dressed in a black pencil skirt and a white pinstriped blouse. She was on her way to work.

"I'm Michaela. I'm here to take you home." I extend my hand a little further, hoping she'll take it this time.

She points over my shoulder instead. "Who are they?"

When I turn and look, I see about five ghosts gathered around the scene of the accident. A few of them have seen me, and they start walking toward us. Silvery gray and quite a bit more opaque than this new spirit beside me, they range in age from early twenties all the way up to a hunched-over old man.

"Come. We need to go." I try to take her hand, but she pulls away.

"Who are they?" she asks, her voice full of fear as she backs away from them.

"You will become one of them if you don't come with me."

She glances back and forth as the ghosts come closer, and then clutches my hand.

It's not the casual walk to which I'm accustomed. We're running. Actually, *I* am running, and I'm dragging my assignment with me. The ghosts are right at our heels, and they're grabbing at us. They don't understand. I can't take them with me now. Their time came and went.

Their behavior strikes me as odd. Normally, ghosts don't give me the time of day. Most of them have chosen to stay. Even those who haven't stayed by choice seem to instinctually know I'm not their ticket home. Once a spirit is rooted to the Earth, a Reaper can't change that for them, no matter how much they are drawn to me.

But these ghosts accept nothing. They didn't choose this, and they're not taking it lying down. They've found me, and they want to go with me.

More than once, my assignment looks back as I drag her into the mists. I keep running, long after there's a need, and her memories fly by us. I don't pay attention to them or even let her take comfort in them. By the time I finally come to a stop, she is shaken. She tries to pull her hand away from me, but I hold firm.

"Just let me get my bearings," she says, but I don't let go.

"No. If I release you in the mists, you'll become one of them—an unmoored spirit. You must wait until you are home."

She frowns at me. "Where is home?"

"We will find out."

"You don't even know where you're taking me?"

"I know it will be one of two places," I say honestly.

"Jesus. I better not end up in hell. I might not have lived long, but I had a good life... I had such plans, Michaela." She smiles in spite of our circumstances, but she chooses not to elaborate. Her thoughts must have turned back to the ghosts because her face turns serious.

"What happened to them? Why were they chasing us?"

I look back over my shoulder, but there's only mist as far as the eye can see. "I imagine they want to go home too."

Horror fills her face. "Why would we leave them behind? Let's go back for them." The urgency in her voice confirms what I already suspected—the black gate won't be waiting for this one.

"Their chance to go home has come and gone. I can't help

them now. Earth has become their home."

She frowns and turns away from me, naturally driven to walk forward. I walk half a step behind her, trying to give her as much space as my arm will allow. More memories play out while we walk, but she still doesn't seem to pay them any mind. They're all happy—birthdays, family gatherings, successes at work, and her favorite hobbies. I enjoy watching them, even if she doesn't.

"Is it like that for you every time you take someone?" she asks, just before her final memory starts to play.

"No."

"So I'm special?" The word catches me off guard.

"Of course you are special, but not in a bad way." I take her hand in both of mine. "You were just unfortunate. In many ways, I'm afraid."

She snorts. "Seems like I'm having a bad day." Her final memory finishes playing, and I realize we both missed almost the entire thing. All I see before the mists start to clear is her blowing the seeds off a daffodil as a young child. The image makes me smile.

"You have a good heart," I say as I lead her to the white gate. "I'm sorry you've started your journey into eternity this way, but I can guarantee you that things will only improve." She follows me in total awe.

The gates of heaven open in greeting, and two angels are there waiting for her. They have golden hair and white gowns that billow welcomingly around them. They stand with their arms extended out, as if reaching for her, and their huge, white wings stretching behind. At the sight of them, I release a breath I didn't know I was holding. They will keep her safe. She will not end up in that horrible prison with the others.

"Audrey, welcome home." They hold their arms out to her, and she rushes toward them without restraint. I watch her go, and the angels nod at me. Despite the fact that I know she's safe with them, I still stand there watching her make her way to them until she is safely, well, under their wings.

Turning around, I scan the mists, searching for another Reaper. I want to know if the others are having this same problem, but no one is around at the moment. Not wanting to waste time dillydallying, I take a deep breath and head back to Earth.

The rest of my day only gets worse. My productivity is down to an all-time low. Everywhere I go, the ghosts are waiting for me, so I spent most of my day dodging them.

I try hanging back in the mists until the last possible moment, but that doesn't work. It takes too long for my assignment to catch sight of me. I nearly lose him to the ghosts. I try hiding behind anything I can find—shrubs, cars, and desks—but that doesn't work either. As soon as I introduce myself to my assignment, it's over. The ghosts are all over me, as if grasping for their missed opportunity.

With each assignment, the number of ghosts seems to increase. A lot of souls had been left behind, I knew this, but I didn't anticipate them flocking to me. I started with only a handful, but by the end of my workday, that number has doubled. There are at least ten waiting for me each time I touch down on Earth. Ten ghosts versus one Reaper. How do they know where I'll be each time? The only thing I can reason out is that they're drawn to dying people because they know a Reaper will come to collect them.

What's even stranger is that they're not the same ghosts. They're different from one visit to the next. It's staggering.

My day is almost over by the time I arrive at Alvin Welstein's house in a small town near the coast of Alabama. Thankfully, the man I'm collecting has lived a long life, so he should be ready to go. His wife passed years ago, and he's been lonely ever since. He's dying in his own bed, surrounded by their children and grandchildren, in the home they shared for over fifty years. As I climb the steps to his room, I prepare myself for the ghosts I know will be waiting for me. I hear his family members in the dining room, talking quietly over a cup of tea. When I reach the bedroom door, I stop and say a silent prayer. I know what waits for me on the other side, and I can only hope I have the strength to get through it.

As I go through the door, I don't make a sound. I glance nervously at the ghosts that surround my assignment before I speak to him. They aren't looking at him—they're keeping watch for someone. I know it's me, but they haven't spotted me yet.

I go to him as quickly as I can. "Come, Alvin. Aimee is waiting for you." It's not a technique I use often, as there's no way of guaranteeing they will both go to the same place and see each other on the other side. But it's a risk I'm willing to take given the fact that ten ghosts have locked in on me and are closing in around us.

"What's happening?" Alvin asks as he firmly grips my hand. The tremble tells me he's just as frightened as I am.

"They want to go home too."

"Let's bring them along. It might be fun," he says, trying to keep a lighthearted tone, although I can hear fear in the quiver of his voice.

The ghosts approach us menacingly, reaching out with silvery arms, their stone-cold grey eyes staring us down.

"Wait!" they call out to us. "Please." Their voices are as faint as the wind, and the sound shakes some of my terror loose. They don't want to hurt us, at least not directly.

They want my help.

"There are children," Alvin says, his voice horrified.

"I know." My heart breaks. If only they were all old men who have lived long lives on Earth and stuck around to cause trouble for their grandkids. But two of them are kids. Kids who were meant to live in comfort for eternity, but who have instead been left behind to watch their families mourn them. Some will have to witness their families be ripped apart by the tragedy of losing them. And all because a few Reapers aren't doing their jobs.

"We can't leave them," Alvin insists.

"But we must. We can't help them," I say calmly, trying not to let him see my anger and despair.

"I don't accept that," he says, turning away from me. He's remarkably strong for an old man, and he jerks my arm when I refuse to release his hand. "I want to help you. Tell me how to help you," he says to the spirits, but they ignore him. Their eyes are only for me.

He holds out his free arm to a nearby child. "Come with us," he says to her. She's small, maybe four, and one of her hands is balled in a transparent blanket while she sucks her thumb. She doesn't make eye contact with Alvin. Tears spring to my eyes as I look at her. She just stares at me, her eyes filled with fear.

"Come," I force myself to say to Alvin. "Your wife is waiting. If you stay here, you two will be apart for all of eternity."

"Just like these folks are separated from their loved ones?" He keeps staring at the little girl, reaching out for her with desperation.

I don't know what will happen if he touches her. The ghosts are all around us now, within arm's reach of me. Of us. Even if Alvin doesn't touch her, I have no idea how we're going to get out of this.

They grab at me, but their hands just pass through me, sending a rush of sadness through me with each swipe. "I'm sorry," I say through the tears that are now spilling freely from my eyes. "I can't help you. And the longer you keep me here, the more souls will join you."

But they don't want to hear it. They know they don't belong on Earth, and they long to break free.

"Why didn't a Reaper take *me* home?"

"Why is he special?"

"What did I do to deserve this?"

The questions come at me, one after another, each from a different voice, and I bring my hands to my ears, pressing the back of the old man's hand to the side of my head, hoping I can block the sound.

But he pulls our joined hands down. "They deserve to know," he says, but his expression is more sympathetic. "I'm no better than this child. Seems to me she's more deserving of an escort. What's happened?"

I shift my weight, not sure of what to say. There's been no discussion on how to handle this. In fact, I'm not sure it was even an anticipated scenario. I have no idea what to tell these spirits. I have many of the same questions they do.

"If I told you the truth, it wouldn't change your fates," I finally say. "Earth is your home now. I'm so sorry. There's nothing I can do for you." I hold out my hand to the nearest ghost, a teenage boy. He reaches for me, but his hand just passes through mine like all the others have. The sadness in his eyes breaks my heart more, causing me to collapse to the ground.

I look up at him. "Please know I'm working hard to prevent more victims from meeting the same fate."

They are not comforted by this. As ghosts, all they care about is what happened to them. Rarely do I see ghosts congregate together, and even more infrequently do they pay any mind to other ghosts. Desperation has brought these spirits together. And I fear that same desperation will keep me here on Earth with them.

"I need to go. I must take Mr. Weltstein back. All I can say is that I'm sorry." It's not enough, and I know it. But I don't think there's anything I can do for them. I can only wish that things had happened differently.

I feel drained and shattered as I sit at the feet of the ghosts around me. They close the circle around us even tighter. I know I must summon the strength to pass through them, but I'm already so exhausted. The mists lie mere feet away, but I'm not sure I can take us to them. The ghosts have drained my energy and life force. They're trying to get home, and they'll do it any way they can. But they're not working together, which means we still have a chance of getting out of here.

"Stop," Alvin says to the ghosts. "You're hurting her." He holds out his hand, but they pay him no mind. They keep grasping at me, each of them taking a small piece of me for themselves.

I'm fading. I can feel it. All at once, I'm exhausted and scared. My fight-or-flight instinct is in full gear. I'm so tired; I just want to sit here and let it happen. But my heart is racing with fear.

Searching the ghosts' faces as they claw at me, I notice one of them has stopped. He's turned away from the rest. The others follow his gaze, and one by one, they turn to look at something.

Alvin's voice is distant, a mere echo of what I know it should be. "Hang on. Help is here."

Warmth encircles me, and I close my eyes, reveling in the sensation. I have no idea how long they stay closed, but when I open them again, a man I don't recognize is looking deep into my eyes.

"Hello there," he says, his voice as scruffy as his appearance. He has a short, scraggly gray beard to match his thin, gray hair. His untucked flannel shirt and loose-fitting jeans make him look like half lumberjack and half homeless. Upon further examination, I notice he's far too clean to be homeless, so I settle on lumberjack.

His pale blue eyes are kind, and I can tell they see far more than they should. I sit up in a panic.

"Who are you? Why can you see me?" I say as I scoot away from him.

"Name's Wyatt." He kneels down and holds out a hand to me. I shrink back from it, and Alvin puts his arms around me.

"But you let go of my hand, Alvin! How are you not a ghost? What's happening?" I say, panicking. I glance around frantically, taking in the scene around me. I'm on the floor in Alvin's bedroom. The ghosts are gone, but the mists remain. Alvin still has a shot at joining his wife.

"It's all right," Alvin says, nodding. "He's saved you, you know. As far as the ghost thing, I don't know. Time seemed to stop for a moment there, I guess to give you a chance to recover."

I blink at the rough-around-the-edges man in front of me. "*You* saved me? How?"

"Just by doing my thing," he says simply, as if that's supposed to explain everything. Then he gives me a quizzical look. "What's the deal with the influx? Haven't seen this many ghosties wandering around since, well…" He scratches at his beard while he considers the question. "Ever."

"I—" I start to explain, but he hasn't answered any of *my* questions. His smug grin isn't hidden by his ill-groomed beard.

As my energy starts to return, I sit up straighter and fold my arms over my chest. "Answer my questions first if you want me to answer yours."

Alvin chuckles behind me. "You've got your hands full with this one, Wyatt."

Wyatt's eyes sparkle, and he winks at me. "You drive a hard bargain, missy. But fine. I'll tell you who I am." He sits back and folds his legs, getting comfortable on the floor of the old man's room. It gives me the impression it's going to be a long story. Alvin stays behind me, and I'm glad for it. He's a comforting presence, and the hand he claps onto my shoulder imparts warmth.

"I'm a medium. I can see ghosts, talk to them, comfort them, calm them if possible, and relocate them if not." He shrugs. "That's it."

Opening my mouth, I close it again. I expected more, but what he's said explains everything. "I didn't know mediums were a real thing."

"Most aren't."

We sit in a stalemate for a few moments before the rest of my questions fill the empty space in the room.

"And Alvin's family just let you in here alone with their dying father?" I say skeptically.

"No, I used my ladder and climbed in through the window. They don't know I'm here. I'll go out the same way, so they don't suspect anything fishy."

"Nice," I say, wondering about the man who saved me. Who climbs into a window to be near a dead man?

"Hey, if you've got any better ideas, I'm all ears," he says, knowing he's got me.

We sit in silence for several moments while I try to get my head around everything and my thoughts circle back to the ghosts. "How did you distract the ghosts? And where did they go?" I scan the room for any sign of the ghosts and come up empty. We're alone.

"Nope. I answered one for you. Now you answer one for me. What's happening, Reaper? Why so many ghosts?"

He knows what I am. Not only can he see me, but he also

knows me. *How?* But I can tell from his stern but kind expression that he won't answer me until I reciprocate. I lean closer to him, and he does the same, as if we're a couple of kids sharing secrets with each other.

"Something's very wrong."

"I gathered that."

I straighten. "Do you want to hear it or not?"

He chuckles and nods. "My apologies."

"It started with the surprises—people who weren't supposed to be taken to their final homes for decades. Suddenly, their names were on our lists to be taken *now*. It added to the workload, and we struggled to keep up. Soon after, a Reaper disappeared. Some Reapers have refused to work because of the 'danger,' resulting in an influx of 'ghosties,' as you call them." I can't help glancing around again, searching for them. It's only then I notice Alvin hasn't changed a single thing about the room since I came to collect his wife. I remember all the humans I've helped. The number is tremendous, but they're all special in some way. Aimee is no exception.

The same floral-print quilt is on the bed, the same pictures hang from the walls, the same trinkets are on the dresser, and her makeup still rests untouched on the antique vanity in the corner. The thought of his love for her warms me, as does the fact that he still has a chance to be reunited with her.

But I still have questions for this medium. "How do you know who I am?"

"Well, I don't know that I know *who* you are. I know *what* you are."

"How?" I press, a small amount of irritation seeping into my voice.

"Honey, I've been doing this a long time. When you spend this much time around the dead, you learn things. I know about Reapers. A few of the spirits who chose not to go with you told me about you folks long ago. That fella behind you is a bit too normal to be a Reaper, so I figured you were the one workin' today."

Alvin smiles. "I've always liked being normal."

It's too much for me. A medium who knows what I am…? Does he know anything else?

"What else do you know?"

He shrugged. "What specifically are you lookin' for?"

"Nothing, I guess. And everything. This is unprecedented. I have no idea how to proceed."

He smiled. "I imagine you ought to take Mr. Alvin here home and be done with it. Especially if you're behind on your work. Best not be sitting here on your laurels," he says, barely holding back a laugh.

He's teasing me. In spite of myself, I smile at him. "Where did the ghosts go?"

"They were attracted to your heavenly energy. So I gave them something else to go after. When they get frenzied like that, they're a bit like zombies. Single-minded, simple beings. I just had to give them something else to focus on. A different, stronger source of energy."

It seems simple, but I know it isn't. "Easy as that?"

"Easy as that."

I stare at him, raising an eyebrow. He chuckles again and lifts his hands in surrender. "Fine. They're in the van, over that way." He nods over my shoulder, and I go to the window. Sure enough, there's an unmarked white van with a trailer attached to the back.

"You fit ten ghosts into that van?"

"Well, some are in the trailer. Ghosts are surprisingly compact," he adds with a shrug. "Ghosties can pass through just about anything, but the van is specially equipped to hold them. Think of an electromagnetic field. It's not exactly the same, but you get the idea. As long as the field is active, they'll be contained inside."

I shake my head, not sure what to do with all this information.

"Well, I hope your friends come back to work soon, missy."

"Michaela," I say, offering my name to him as an olive branch.

"Michaela," he says. "There's only one of me, and I can't be everywhere. I was lucky to come across poor Alvin here."

"How *did* you find us?" Alvin asks.

"I was out drivin' and suddenly had the urge to take a look at some of these old houses. Not sure where that came from. Then I came across this place. I knew something was up when I sensed the size of the gathering. Ghosts are selfish creatures. They don't listen to each other at all… Honestly, I'm not convinced they can even *see* each other, which makes for a lonely existence if you think about it. But that's why they don't have much of a reason to congregate. I knew something had drawn them all together, and whatever it was would lose the fight. So I pulled over and found you two."

Did the hand of God steer him here, or was it mere coincidence? But if I've learned anything recently, it's that coincidences are unlikely at best.

Wyatt thought for a moment before asking me, "Has the missing Reaper been found?"

I shake my head, and he frowns. "Something fishy is going on, mi…" He stops and corrects himself. "Michaela. And like I said, I'm only one guy. What're the odds you'll need to pick someone up in my neck of the woods again? What will you do next time?"

I frown. "I don't know."

"I can't trap the ghosts forever. It's hard on them. They'll dissipate if I just keep them contained. I don't want to be responsible for that, even if they're unhappy with their current situation."

"I don't have any other solutions for you right now, Wyatt. But believe me, if we learn something, you'll be the first person I tell," I say, glad to have an ally on this side.

He stands to leave, reaching out his hand for me. I stand too and shake it. "Michaela. Best of luck to you."

"You too, Wyatt. Until we meet again." I feel certain this isn't the last time our paths will cross.

He nods and walks to the door.

"Wyatt?" He turns to me. "Thank you."

"Any time, missy." He smiles out of one side of his mouth

and leaves Alvin and me to our business.

"Well, shall we go see your wife?" I ask him.

"I'd like that," he says as we begin walking into the mists.

Alvin was my last for the day. Under normal circumstances, I would've worked through the night to make up for our losses, but we have to save Webber. We can't leave him in hell for another day. Who knows what will become of him in there. Even if we succeed in rescuing him, he may not recover from the torture if he's left there too long.

I shuffle back to the naming room, where the dissenters are lounging around a circular table with their feet propped up. They're laughing and carrying on. A sudden rush of anger gives me energy and makes me stand up a little straighter. I storm over to them.

"*You* nearly cost me my life today," I say, gracing them all with my most withering stare.

One or two of them look up with a surprised expression, but Heth steadfastly ignores me.

"I was attacked by ghosts today, and it was all because of *your* selfish behavior. The only danger out there is the one *you've* created."

Heth smiles condescendingly at me, but the others look a little uncomfortable.

"What were you doing around ghosts in the first place? Sounds to me like you endangered yourself," Heth says while examining his fingernails.

"They sought *me* out. They knew they weren't supposed to be there. At first, there were only a handful of them, but as the day went on, more and more gathered around each of the souls I was supposed to collect. They wanted to know why the people on my list were more special than they were. Why someone didn't come for them. And the way the children looked at me—" I stop. A hand squeezes my shoulder.

I recognize the small fingers as Miette's. Turning, I hug her, so relieved to see that she's returned in one piece. Given her gentle nature, I was most worried about her.

"You're okay," I breathe.

"Barely." She turns to face the group. "It was the same for me. Is anyone else back yet?"

One of the dissenters shakes his head with a grave expression on his face. But the rest of the Reapers do eventually return. By some miracle, the ghosts haven't succeeded in claiming any of us today. Once we're all gathered, Ryker walks silently to the platform to address us.

"Today was a needlessly dangerous day. I'm sorry. I'm working on defenses for you. Unfortunately, due to complications and a lack of participation…" He eyes the dissenters. Only Heth is still smiling. The others are hanging their heads. "17,632 ghosts have been created in the last two days. That's almost twenty thousand ghosts who are going to try to absorb your life force and use it to go home. Be on your guard."

This news causes us all to shift uncomfortably, even the dissenters. A few clear their throats. We look away from Ryker and exchange uneasy glances.

I clear my throat. "I was saved by a human today."

Silence reigns in the room, and Ryker looks closely at me. "A human?"

"A medium. Or so he called himself. He could see the ghosts. Just happened to be driving by when I was collecting my last soul for the day." I eye Ryker, wondering if he sent Wyatt, or if the order came from higher up. "He saved me."

"He can control them?" Ryker narrows his gaze at me.

"For a time, anyway. Not indefinitely."

Ryker nods. "Valuable information. Thank you, Michaela."

The room is silent for a few beats while they absorb what I've just revealed.

"There's more," he says, and we brace ourselves for what's to come. I can guess the news from his grim expression, and my stomach rolls. I'm not sure I can handle this today.

"A new name has appeared on the list for tomorrow. Another surprise."

A collective gasp tears through the group. Even the dissenters are upset by the news.

"Michaela, I need you to retrieve this one." I nod. Despite the fact that I collected the last surprise, I feel it's my duty to make sure this one makes it to his or her final destination.

I wait patiently for the name, and it hits me like a freight train.

Lily Moynagh. A child.

EIGHT

"No." I breathe. "This can't be right. Not a child," I plead with Ryker.

But I can tell from his stiff posture there's nothing he can do, and he's as unhappy about this news as I am. "The name was clear when it appeared, although I don't disagree that there's been a mistake."

"But she's a child. None of the other surprises were this young."

"I know," he says as he climbs down from the platform. I follow him desperately, like some sad puppy looking for reassurance.

"Do you? This can't be happening, sir. Not a child. Not like this. The parents…" It doesn't matter that I don't know who they are. I can't shake the image of them clinging to their daughter as I steal her from them before her time. It fuels the anger building in me.

"It's needless," I insist. "How is this any different from what Penn was banished for? It's an unnecessary loss of life," I say, and all motion and chatter ceases around me.

Ryker turns to me. "It's not. And whoever is responsible will not be given the luxury of banishment. That I can assure you of."

"Is Nathair doing this?" someone in the back of the crowd asks.

"We don't know. All we know for sure is that a new name popped up today after several days of silence." He pauses and looks at each of our faces in turn. "Now, more than ever, I need you *all* to join together to help us fight what's happening. Selfishness will no longer be tolerated."

"What does that mean?" Heth demands, clearly irritated by the threat.

Ryker crosses the room and approaches him until the two men are nearly nose to nose—or they would be if Ryker weren't so much bigger. "It means make your choice now, before my forgiveness is outside of your reach." With that, he turns abruptly and leaves.

When the glass doors close, I feel like they're closing on my heart. A child.

"A child," Miette whispered behind me. "How will you bring yourself to do it? I'm not sure I could."

"I must. Or she will become one of the ghosts." The thought fans the flames of my anger. "Unless…"

I walk away, increasing my pace with each step. One man could stop all of this with a single word. And that little girl's name is all the motivation I need to ask Him. Maybe He has a plan, but how can it include the early death of a child who was supposed to live a long, full life? How can that possibly be good and perfect? With my world unraveling around me, I feel like I can no longer depend on His plan. In fact, for the first time, I find myself doubting it.

Miette jogs to keep up with me. "Where are you going?"

"To see someone who can put a stop to this, once and for all," I say, leaving her behind me as I race to see God.

I pound on the solid white door rather unceremoniously. It opens so suddenly that my fist is left hanging in the air. Although this is my first visit to God's office, we all know where it is. We're shown during training, and it's assumed we won't come here unless summoned. But today, I don't care about assumptions. I care about getting answers.

His office is rather barren, and the white-on-white décor doesn't help. Maybe He's going for a minimalist approach.

I march through the door and approach His desk. He's sitting there, writing something down, his glasses perched neatly at the end of his nose. "Please, sit down if you'd like, Michaela." He doesn't look up when he speaks. The deep, soothing voice of God does nothing to calm me, though perhaps that's because I'm too wrapped up in my own problems to let that happen.

"I would prefer to stand," I say, much too fired up to settle into the plush white armchair across from Him.

"That's fine. I'll just be a moment," he says. In all honesty, I didn't really expect Him to see me at all. He's obviously very busy—he is, after all, *God*—and I just stormed into his office. He has no obligation to hear my rant. These thoughts are enough to give me foresight to wait—not so patiently—until He's ready for me.

After what feels like an eternity, but is probably only a few moments, he finally puts down his pen and removes his glasses. Resting them on the desk in front of him, he looks up at me. "What can I do for you, my dear Reaper?" he asks. His voice is soothing, but I resist its effect on my nerves, clinging to my anger like a lifeboat. One I want to use to save Lily.

"A child?" I demand.

"Can you be more specific?" he says. "There are lots of children on Earth at the moment."

"I know You know who I mean. The newest surprise?"

"Ah. Yes. *That* child."

Suddenly, my rage turns to sorrow, and I sink down into the armchair in tears. "How can You allow this? I can't possibly take a child before her time. Don't you know how devastated her parents will be? They won't even fully grasp the senselessness of her death. It's the worst possible crime against humanity, and I'm supposed to perpetrate it?" The tears are flowing freely by now, and God rises from his seat and comes around his desk to kneel in front of me. That takes me aback—*God* is kneeling in front of me.

The sheer averageness of his appearance strikes me in that moment. Short, brown hair, brown eyes, a blue button-up shirt, and khaki pants. He looks so totally... well, normal. He could be anyone. And maybe that's the point. He *is* everyone.

He covers my hands with His, and I look into his eyes. They are filled with compassion and pain, as if my tears are His own. "Michaela, my dear. Of course I understand. I feel their pain even more than you do, if you can believe it." Pulling me from my seat, He leads me to the back of his office. He pushes a spot that looks no different from any other in the white wall, but a hidden door opens, revealing a beautiful garden beyond it.

There are tall, willowy trees behind rows of short, flowering bushes in colors I've never seen on Earth. They are such a contrast to the white office that it's a bit jarring at first. The trees stretch above us and form a beautiful canopy, and the slight breeze carries the scent of lavender. We walk hand in hand through the garden, not speaking until I can't stand it anymore.

"Is this the Garden of Eden?"

He chuckles a little, but it's not condescending at all. "No. This place is just for me. The Garden existed only on Earth."

I nod, feeling a little stupid, although I know that wasn't His intention. It's just so lovely. I know intuitively that this level of beauty exists nowhere else, neither in the heavens, nor on Earth.

While we are walking, we pass a dark forest. It's such a contrast to the bright garden that the question is pulled out of me of its own accord. "What's that?" I nod toward the dark woods.

"That's the Forest of Confusion. The humans have many questions. Many injustices they don't understand. Many things they simply can't wrap their heads around. Some think I don't hear their demands for answers, but I do. They make up that forest."

"Do You ever go in there? It looks frightening."

He's smiling as he looks down at me. "Dealing with the humans can be scary business, can't it?" Thinking back on my encounters with the ghosts, I nod.

He says nothing more on the topic, and we continue our

walk through His corner of heaven. I've lost all concept of time in this beautiful place. In some ways it feels like I've spent my whole life here, walking down the path at my feet, and yet it also feels like only a few moments have passed. Soon, we come upon a creek. We follow it as we walk, and it gradually opens to a river before dumping into a huge ocean.

"This ocean is made of the tears of my humans. So many tears," God says, and the sadness in His voice makes me drop to my knees. I sink into the sugary white sand, feeling an overwhelming urge to walk out into the ocean and never surface again. What is the point of so much suffering? The waves from this ocean of tears lap at my knees, and I am powerless to hold them back. In fact, my own tears flow freely, adding to the ocean's depths.

"I feel the pain of the humans as if it's my own," He says as He looks out across the waters. No land is in sight. All I see is vast, open ocean.

I feel stupid. Of course He understands. I was ignorant to even suggest He didn't. How could He not understand what His creations are going through?

"I'm sorry." It's the only thing I can think to say.

He says nothing. Simply stares out into the ocean.

"What if I refuse to collect her? She may be spared a worse fate," I say. The thought of such a young girl being trapped in the prison of souls makes me cringe. But neither can I stomach the thought of her lingering behind to torture not only herself, but also her poor family. "The souls in the prison are dying. Fading away to nothingness. I can't let that happen to a child."

"Diligence," He says quietly. "You must be diligent. I need you now more than ever, Michaela. I know you can get to the bottom of what's happening. And I need you to do it so I can hold someone accountable for these crimes. Your fight isn't over." He turns away from the ocean of tears and looks at me.

"Regardless of what you choose to do for Lily, your fight hasn't even started yet."

A chill runs down my spine and I rub my arms, trying to banish it. He reaches out His hand to help me up, and I take it.

Together, we walk away from the ocean of tears.

"Be strong now, Michaela," he says. "Be the creation I made you to be." Then everything dissolves away and I am left alone just outside his office, with no concept of how long I was in God's corner of heaven.

NINE

The transition is so jarring that it steals my breath for a moment. I lean a hand against the nearby wall and take a moment to catch my breath. Never in my entire existence have I seen that kind of beauty. Being back in the heavens seems dull in comparison, even though I know it's not.

Be strong now. Be the creation I made you to be. I wasn't made to be a Reaper. I was made for something more. His words echo in my mind as I try to steel myself for the night ahead. "My fight isn't over," I say to myself out loud in the empty hallway. I must rally all my strength and move forward.

But when I think about everything that must be done, it threatens to overwhelm me. *Small bites*, I remind myself. Take it in small bites. What's the first thing that needs to be done? Webber. We have to go back to hell and get Webber.

Dread fills my stomach until I think it will spill out of my mouth. But instead of shrinking back from this task, I straighten and march toward my quarters where we arranged to meet. It's the only way I can help ensure a better future, one where this isn't happening, one where children are no longer in danger of losing their existence.

They're waiting for me again in my room. Their expressions tell me they can sense something's happened.

Galenia rushes over to me. "What's wrong?" she asks as she puts her arm around me and ushers me into my room.

I decide to start at the beginning. "I was attacked by ghosts today," I state. As if it were no big thing. As if I weren't in danger of losing my very existence.

"You *what?*" Penn asks, rushing up to me too.

"The ghosts are piling up on Earth, making my job a bit… challenging." I smile at Galenia, trying to assure her I'm fine.

"Is that why you're late?" Horatia eyes me, as if she instinctually knows there's more to the story than I'm letting on.

"Not entirely, no," I say carefully as I make my way to the couch and sit down.

I shouldn't have done it. The weight of the ghosts, of Lily, of the garden and the ocean of tears, of Webber, of… *everything* presses me down into the cushions. I want to stay there forever.

"So, why are you late?" Penn asks cautiously as he watches me.

The tears threaten again as I look at him, but I manage to hold them back. "A new name popped up today. Another surprise."

They're all frowning, and I haven't even told them the worst of it.

"Well, we'll just have to work quickly tonight. Maybe we'll figure this situation out tonight. If we're lucky, you won't have to collect them tomorrow," Horatia says with confidence, as if she knows without a shadow of a doubt that it's as simple as that.

They're standing around me, ready to take action. As if the human behind the name isn't important. And to them, it's not. They don't know her. *I* don't even know her yet.

"Who is it?" Penn asks reluctantly, his voice heavy with dread.

"It's a child."

"What?" Galenia asks, clearly shattered by the news. She sinks down into the couch next to me and stares off ahead of us, hands folded neatly in her lap.

"What about the guards at the weaving room? How did someone get past them?" Penn demands. "Maybe it's the Weaver..." I can tell his mind is working a thousand miles a minute, searching for a solution, a way out of this mess.

It's so difficult to get out the next words, but they need to be said. "I'm supposed to collect her first thing tomorrow." I look over at Penn, who seems to be filled with a combination of rage and sorrow.

"What can we do?" Horatia asks.

"Save Webber. Free the souls in the prison. Hope that's enough to stop whatever's happening," I say. I have no other ideas, so I can only pray it's enough.

Penn gives voice to my darkest fears. "What if it isn't enough? What if whoever's doing this doesn't even know about the prison? They're just cutting threads, happy as can be, with no concept of the consequences? If that's the case, the prison will keep filling up until we find the culprit."

"Guards were posted at the weaving room not two days ago, Penn. I wouldn't want to trifle with those Archangels. This goes deeper than someone just cutting threads," Horatia offers.

"Well, it seems like someone trifled with them and got away with it," he says. I can tell he's not convinced.

He looks to me earnestly. "You can't take a child before her time. Before she's even had the smallest chance to fulfill her fate, whatever it is. Her parent's fates are surely intertwined with hers. The cascading consequences are absolutely dire. You must see that you can't do this." He says it as if it's a truth. One I must abide.

"I can't leave her, either," I say. "She will die tomorrow whether I come for her or not. If I leave her, she'll become a ghost, and she'll torture her poor family until they all die. Then she'll be left on Earth alone. Is that what she deserves?"

He frowns. "Those can't be our only choices."

"For now, they are. If we don't fix this, the names will keep coming, and the situation will only get worse," I say, sounding more confident than I am. I reach for his hand, and he lets me take it despite his outrage at the situation. As I stand up, I feel energized and slightly more ready to face the night ahead. Maybe, just maybe, we can handle this. "There's work to be done," I say.

The Fates all look back at me with grave expressions. I say a silent prayer that we will succeed tonight as we file quietly out of my room and off to the gates of hell once more.

Once we're on the other side of the gate, we don't speak. There's nothing to discuss. We're all focused on our mission. We *have* to succeed.

Part of me feels a little bitter. We shouldn't be here. Not again. Not so soon. But I know that's just hell taking its toll on me, feeding on my emotions. *Diligence*, God said. That's what I need. Not wallowing. *Diligence*. I repeat it in my head as we walk through the outskirts of hell, and the mantra makes me stronger.

Our cover story is the same as it was before—I'm bringing the others on another tour of hell. We can only hope we won't run into the same demon we saw yesterday. The odds are slim, and I'm willing to bet on them. If we do see him, we'll demand the release of our friend. No cloak-and-dagger stuff—just let him go and we'll be on our way. Of course, we'll still plan on making a short detour to the prison, but he doesn't need to know that part.

Either way, it's a problem for my future self. My current goal is to get to Webber, and I can only hope there's a minimum amount of complications. But I know it's a foolish thought; hope doesn't exist here in the depths of hell.

As we wander the dark caverns, Penn finally breaks our silence. "How come this prison couldn't be on the outskirts of heaven? We could be wandering in a much more pleasant place. And Webber would be living it up! He wouldn't even want us to come back for him," he says. I think he means it as a joke, but no one laughs. It feels impossible to laugh here.

I lead them through another turn and down a dank corridor, trying to find my way to the hall of black doors where we left

Webber, but I'm quickly realizing I don't recognize this area. I stop and glance over my shoulder. It all looks the same to me. We were all so upset when we left Webber here last night. My feet led the way to the door seemingly of their own accord. Now, it seems like an eternity has passed since we were last here. My soul is stretched too thin. I'm tired, and it's showing.

As I glance back and forth, I come to a terrible conclusion. I'm lost in the depths of hell with everyone I hold most dear.

TEN

Penn picks up on my distress right away. "Okay," he whispers to me. "Let's not panic. The holding area was on the outskirts of hell, not that far from the prison. I think we went too far. Let's go back a bit." He turns, and pushes through the girls. They turn and follow him. I go to the back of the group, following a Spinner through the depths of hell. It feels so wrong on so many levels.

I should've gone straight to the prison and made my way from there. I could never forget the location of that horrible place. Moments into this mission, I've already forgotten my main directive. *Diligence*.

While I try not to despair, Penn manages to guide us back to recognizable territory. Before long, I know exactly where we are.

"I recognize this skull." Although there are many skulls buried in the walls of the caves of hell, this one stands out to me. It's missing teeth—one tooth on top and one on the bottom, making its grin grotesquely comical. Almost like a jack-o-lantern.

It rests at the crest of a fork in the caverns. When we pop out from the tunnel, we're left with two options. One leads to the prison, so I can infer that the other leads to Webber.

"We should stick together until we find Webber. Then we'll go from there, okay?" I say, hoping I sound authoritative enough that they won't question me. Penn isn't convinced.

"Why don't you and one of the girls go get Webber, and someone can come with me to the prison?"

Galenia looks back and forth between us. "I think we should stick together. At least until Webber is safe."

Horatia agrees. "I'm sorry, Penn, but unfortunately, Webber is our main objective right now."

"He got himself in that mess," Penn grumbles. "As far as I'm concerned, we have bigger fish to fry." He keeps the anger in his voice just below the surface, and I'm glad for that. Fear, anger, aggression, these emotions are like beacons to the demons, so it's important that we all keep ourselves in check.

"We do have bigger fish to fry. Once he's safe," I say. We need Penn's single-minded focus to help us accomplish our mission, but we can't very well leave Webber behind.

Galenia steps in. "What happened to coming back for him?" she asks, looking at him with pleading eyes.

Reluctantly, he relents. We go—one of us rather begrudgingly—down the hall to the sorting rooms where we last saw Webber. I count the doors as I go, hoping beyond hope that I'm counting right. Everything is so foggy from yesterday, and it all happened so fast. I try hard to play the moment over in my mind. "It was the fifth door on the right, right?" I ask. No one answers.

"Let's try it and see." I take a breath and open the door. None of the doors in hell are locked. There's nowhere for the souls to go, and most don't even try to escape. They don't even see it as an option. Demons and Reapers are the only ones who know the doors aren't locked. Surely Webber thinks he's trapped, just as the souls do.

The cell is dark, making it impossible to see very far inside. The red glow from the hallway spills inside some, making the darkness retreat to the very back of the cell. This leaves a small area where he could be hiding. "Webber?" I whisper into the darkness. No reply.

"If you're in here, now's not the time for caution." Silence. I sigh and glance back at the others, who are keeping watch in the hall. We haven't seen any demons so far, but I doubt our luck will hold. Taking a risk, I decide to walk the perimeter of the room. I don't want to move on without him if he's right under my nose. But we don't have time to search every cell this way. We still have the prison to address. I pick up my pace as I walk, feeling my way along the wall when I reach the total darkness in the back. I try not to think about what I'm touching as my hand runs over cold, smooth bumps.

I can't accept the fact that he's not here, that they've moved him deeper into hell. My hope to find him fast and move on is withering in the face of the growing idea that we might not find him at all.

As I shuffle forward in the darkness, no one speaks. Slowly, I circle back around to the door, having found the cell empty.

"Maybe I picked the wrong cell," I say, hoping that's true. But here in hell, truths are hard to come by.

No one says anything as Penn and Horatia take the door to the left and Galenia and I take the door to the right. Theirs is another empty space, but mine has someone inside. Unfortunately, it's not our quarry.

"Who are you?" the soul asks, his voice quivering.

I frown sadly at him. I can't help him. "I'm sorry to have disturbed you," I say before shutting the door.

He runs to it and pounds hard, making a tremendous amount of noise. "Please! Don't leave me here! You have to help me!"

Soon, we hear the telltale shuffling of demons approaching. With nowhere else to go, we all duck into Webber's empty cell.

A demon bangs on the cell next door. "Hey," he hollers. His loud voice echoes through the halls. The man immediately stops pounding and goes quiet.

"Don't make me come in there," the demon threatens.

We listen to his steps recede, and even after he's long gone, we sit in the silence and darkness, not quite sure of what to do next.

"We could ask a demon where he went. Tell them we're trainees, and we're curious to know what happened to the soul we brought in yesterday," Horatia suggests.

Although it's not a bad suggestion, I'd rather not seek out the attention of demons. It seems like we'd just be asking for trouble. On the other hand, what better place to hide than out in the open? I waffle for a moment before I land on a decision. "I think we should at least try to find him on our own. Asking a demon can be our last resort," I say.

"The demon yesterday said Webber thought he was better than others. That might narrow down where they brought him. *If* they decided that was his punishable crime. If they chose something else…" I take a deep breath. "He could be anywhere." My mind spins with the possibilities. Hell is broken into many different areas, each focused on punishing a particular set of crimes. We'll never cover all of hell in one night. The search could take more than a lifetime. That's just the nature of hell. You're not meant to leave.

"We shouldn't have left him here," Galenia says.

"We had no choice," Penn says in the darkness. "We had to go or be trapped here right along with him."

"We can't afford to dwell on shouldas and couldas. We need to focus on what we can do now," I say as I squeak the door open, letting a sliver of light into the cell. Poking my head out, I scan the hall in both directions. No one is out there wandering, so I ease my way out and lead the others deeper into hell.

At the end of the corridor, the holding cells taper off, and the walkway opens to an expansive stone room that maintains the same creepy, red glow. The smell of sulfur is even worse as we move deeper into hell, and I fear I may never get it out of my nose, let alone my hair. There's a tall but seemingly controlled flame in front of us. It travels the length of the room, extending at least three feet above my head.

"What is this?" Horatia asks.

"It's the maze," I say. "It's where those who've misled others for one reason or another are trapped. They're doomed to go round and round inside for all eternity, never finding their way out."

"That's terrible," Galenia says.

"It's meant to mirror what they've done in life to others." I say, my tone matter of fact. As Reapers, we're taught not to dwell on the punishments. They are carefully crafted, calculated, and assigned. The punishments assigned to human souls are earned through a misspent lifetime on Earth. Nothing more, nothing less.

"Do you think he could be in there?" Horatia asks.

"Not really. But if he's there and we don't look for him, we'll always regret it," I say.

"He did sort of mislead us about his skills as a Spinner. He always said he'd be a better Spinner than Penn, and we all know how that turned out," Horatia says. Webber always coveted Penn's job, saying he'd do a superior job to the best Spinner in history. Well, when Penn was banished, he finally got what he wanted. But it turns out he was much better suited to life as a weaver, although I'm not sure he would admit that. Not even now.

Even if we manage to rescue him from hell, I have no idea what his future will hold. We all know he'll be replaced as the Spinner as soon as a suitable candidate can be found. And someone has already replaced him as Weaver. So he can't go back to his previous job either. It's a problem for a day when our problems are more superficial than they are today. First, we have to get him out of this dreadful place.

"Well, there's only one way to find out," I say, gazing at the wall of fire.

"You're going in there?" Galenia asks, clearly horrified.

I laugh. The sound feels out of place, and it echoes throughout the caverns. Clapping my mouth shut, I listen for the footsteps of demons running toward the odd noise in their home.

When I feel safe—well, as safe as I can feel in hell—I shake my head. "No, I'm not going in there. But if Horatia stands on Penn's shoulders, she should be able to get a good view of who's inside. Just try to be discreet. If any of the souls see you, they'll want help."

Horatia and Penn are the two tallest members of our group. The fire is taller than I am, but their combined height should allow them to see past it.

As she's climbing up onto Penn's shoulders, Horatia says, "There's so much fire, but there's no smoke or heat."

"These are the flames of hell," I explain. "They will only burn or choke those they're meant to burn and choke. The souls inside have probably long since moved away from them. The fire is only on the outermost edge, to discourage escape. The souls who travel through it think they've gained refuge in the corridors of the maze, but things only get worse for them the further they go. Spikes jut out at them from all angles so they can't sit down, horrific creatures crawl on them, people chase them... basically anything that keeps the soul moving constantly, without rest."

No one says anything. It's a terrible fate, but there's nothing any of us can do about it, so Penn hoists Horatia up.

They tumble on the first try. "This dress is a bit... cumbersome, Michaela," Horatia says. "How do you get anything done in it?"

I smile. "Carefully."

She snorts and tries again, hoisting herself up on Penn's shoulders. "Helpful." She's quiet for a long moment as she searches the maze. Finally, she whispers, "I see someone close by, but it's not Webber."

Before she can climb down, I implore her to keep looking. "Do you see anyone else?"

"Yes. There are so many souls inside..." Her voice is low, and her face has lost its color. She's despairing. One by one, that toxic emotion will take all of us if I let it.

"Don't lose hope now. We *will* find him," I say, desperately trying to give her some hope in this hopeless place.

"How? There are too many to count, let alone identify."

"Should we call out to him?" Penn asks as he holds onto Horatia's ankles.

Galenia wrinkles her nose. "I don't think we should draw attention to ourselves. If we're discovered here, we'll be no good to him."

"What do you think, Michaela?" Penn asks as he shifts his

weight, balancing Horatia carefully.

"I don't think he's in there. And if he is… he's as good as lost to us anyway," I say darkly. There's no way we could save him from the maze. There's one way in, but there's no way out. Truthfully, though I don't tell them as much, we needn't have looked. If we found him in there, we'd only be able to say goodbye. He wouldn't have heard us, but at least we would have had closure.

We're all silent for a moment while Horatia climbs down.

"What now?" she asks once her feet are firmly back on the ground.

"We go deeper into hell."

ELEVEN

We walk the perimeter of the maze for what feels like an eternity, and I start to worry about how much time we have left. We can't be caught here during work hours. If we are, Lily will be left behind to become one of Earth's lonely shades, and the Reapers will be short another hand. Not to mention the fact that all the Fates will be lost. The creation of human life will come to a complete and total standstill.

Of course, trying to calculate what time it is in hell is nearly impossible. It's designed to feel infinite and excruciating.

"We need to watch the time," I say as we finally make it to the other end of the maze. The room starts to narrow in, leading to another corridor. I'm not looking forward to going back to the cramped caverns, but at least it'll lead us away from the maze.

I pause in the entryway to the next section, listening hard for wandering demons. When I hear nothing, I press forward. It's an odd area, and the group has a hard time processing what we're seeing.

The long hallway we're walking down is lined with cells on either side. The cells all have old-fashioned wooden doors, embedded with small windows covered by iron bars. It's reminiscent of an old dungeon, save for the red glow that bathes everything in demonic light.

Taking a divide-and-conquer approach, we each choose a cell and peer inside. There are tremendous amounts of people in each. But on further inspection, there is only one solid soul in each of them. The others are a bit transparent. The soul at the center of the mass I'm watching is holding his ears. He's being verbally assaulted by the others. They're asking questions, placing demands, telling stories, and jabbering continuously. It's an unceasing hum of sound.

The reflections are tugging at him, pulling his hands away from his ears, demanding to be heard, to be heeded, but not necessarily to be answered. When he relents and brings his hands down, the reflections only press in harder and speak louder.

Despite the fact that we've delved further into hell than most heavenly beings ever do, each new form of torture is difficult to absorb. We stand at those first cells and watch the souls trapped inside, helpless to save them. I remember seeing this section of hell centuries ago on my tour, but I haven't been back since. Still, the memory is fresh. The sight of those tortured souls isn't easily forgotten.

"What is the larger message here?" Galenia asks. "Those in the maze were left to wander after misleading folks their whole lives. What have these people done?"

Penn speaks up before I can, which surprises me. "I read about this in the Keepers' books. This punishment is for those who thrived on attention, demanding things from everyone around them, talking constantly about themselves and their own needs without ever expecting a response. These were the souls who always ensured the focus was constantly on them." He says it without taking his eyes off the soul inside the cell he's peering into.

"It's not necessarily their only crime," I add. "Just the one the demons deemed most effective to punish."

"What does that mean?" Horatia asks.

"Each human is unique, and so is their punishment," I try to explain as we walk, peeking into each cell, searching for our lost Spinner. "Some humans who were violent toward others, murderers, rapists, things like that, aren't necessarily hurt by violence themselves. In fact, they enjoy it. So the demons must find another way to torture them. Perhaps a man like that sought validation from his mother as a child and never got it? He might be trapped with a reflection of her, only to be ignored for all eternity. Although there are general areas of hell where many souls are receiving the same treatment, the demons will assure you each punishment is specially tailored to the soul. They take great pride in the care that goes into the soul's time here."

I pause as I stand on my tiptoes and peek into the next cell. Not him. "Honestly, they devote just as much time to the souls here in hell as they do in heaven. The care is just... different."

"Different is one way to put it," Horatia says as she checks the cell next to me.

In the distance, I hear footsteps and a thunderous sound that can only be a pair of demons laughing. They're coming straight for us. With nowhere to go, we each duck into our respective cells. After all, they're not locked. It doesn't seem like the best plan, but we're out of options.

After soundlessly shutting the door, I sink down to the floor just below the window. Should the demon look inside, I don't want to be seen. I wish I could tell the others to do the same, but I can only hope they're smart enough to stay hidden.

The demons wander past the cells, dragging something along the doors, making a terribly loud banging noise. It's that sound that draws the attention of the soul inside the cell I've snuck into.

He locks eyes with me, and it's obvious he knows I'm not a reflection. Somehow, he understands I don't belong here. He pushes through the crowd of reflections, and they follow him, bringing their racket with them. Louder and louder and louder they come.

Automatically, my hands rise to my ears, and I can no longer hear anything from outside. I have no idea where the demons are, let alone if they've moved on.

"Please," the soul pleads with me. He's a businessman in appearance—middle aged and clean cut—except for his loosened tie and disheveled hair, which I can only assume are results of his imprisonment.

I don't respond to him, figuring it's best not to engage. Risking a glance up at the window, I start to stand for a better view, but the very distinct smell of rotting flesh makes me sink slowly back down.

"Hey," the demon in the hallway shouts as he bangs on the door with some kind of object. "Keep it down in there. Get back away from the door."

"But there's someone in here with me," the spirit says, throwing caution to the wind.

"Yes. There are a lot of people in there with you, I imagine. Get back away from the door," he insists.

Faintly, I can hear the other demon having a similar conversation at another cell. I can only hope the soul in there is cowed into silence.

My heart pounds so loudly I fear it may give me away.

The soul crouches down in front of me, and the ghosts pile on top of him, screaming their incessant demands. "Please. Show yourself to him. Maybe you can get us both out of here," he shouts.

The demon bangs on the door again, silencing the ghosts for just an instant. "Don't make me come in there. Get away from the door."

The other demon joins him. *I'm sunk*, I think. They're sure to find me in here. I try to come up with an excuse for why I'm inside, but I know my ideas are all thin... The best story I can think of is that I'm conducting some sort of inspection.

The door swings inward, pushing me between it and the wall.

"I'm *not* screwing around here, bub. Get away from the damned door," the demon says. His partner must be leaning against the door, because it's absolutely crushing me. I can barely take a breath, and suddenly, I'm glad I was crouching. At least I have more padding. I try to wiggle my arms up to cushion my head a bit better, but they're totally pinned. After I catch a glimpse of the back of the demon's partner, I freeze in place. It's a Warden. Dressed in jeans and a freshly pressed button-down shirt, he looks oddly human in this world of monsters. But that's the Warden's appeal. They often buddy up with the souls inside these cells, giving them false hope—something that will only torture them more in the long run. The Wardens are managers of a sort. If this one finds me, I will never see the mists again. Forgiveness and second chances are not phrases that exist in hell.

The soul inside the cell isn't deterred by the Warden. The reflections have disappeared for the moment. He scoots away from the door, but he points right at me and looks me in the eye. I silently plead with him for discretion, but he ignores it. Or maybe he's beyond understanding. "She's there."

That single heartbeat drags on for an eternity. The trapped man sits, leaning back on one hand, his other hand extended toward me in an accusing gesture. The first demon towers over him, burned flesh hanging from his body, huge black wings extending from his back. If he turns and sees me, it's over.

Your fight isn't over yet. I hear God's words echoing in my mind. *Don't give up so easily*, I chide myself. *It's not the end until you decide to stop fighting.* I try to take a deep, cleansing breath, but it's enough to remind me of my situation. I'm pinned behind the door, just inches from a demon. A short, silent gasp will have to do.

"I think it's time for a transfer," the demon says as he looks over his right shoulder at his friend, the Warden. I freeze, hoping neither of them can see me. I feel like the fear coursing through me is a lighthouse drawing the demons' red gaze, but I can't seem to calm my pounding heart.

"I couldn't agree more," the Warden agrees. He must have moved away from the door, because the pressure eases a little, revealing more of me. Together, they pull the man's spirit from the cell. He fights them, giving me time to gather the bottom of my dress and cover myself in the darkness behind the door, using it as a makeshift shield to blend into the wall. Or that's my hope, anyway

I don't risk peeking out at them. I'm completely wrapped in the skirt of my dress, and I don't want to draw attention to myself by doing something as stupid as moving…or even breathing.

I hold my breath as I listen to the nearby struggle. The two demons seem to be teasing the soul, laughing at his attempts to get away from them.

"I don't see anyone at all. Do you?" the Warden asks.

This is it. The moment of truth. I can tell from the clarity of their voices that they're facing me. The door isn't concealing me at all anymore. It opened enough in my scramble that I'm totally exposed, save for the cover of my gown.

"Nope. All I see is a damned fool," the demon says.

They laugh again as they open the door a little wider, slamming it against me, and carry the poor soul out of the cell. They close it behind them, thank God. The soul puts up quite a fight judging from the sound of the scuffle, and eventually, the demons get tired of it. I hear a thump, followed by the soul's silence. His presence in the hall is now covered up by the incessant murmuring of voices coming from all sides of the hallway.

"Finally," the Warden says.

"Aw, but I was having fun with him."

"I was getting tired of his struggling. He has no fear of us. That needs to be corrected immediately." The dark tone of his voice makes me wince. I've caused this soul further pain, further torture.

Their footsteps and voices fade as they carry the man down the hall away from us.

I'm frozen by fear and left in total silence inside the cell. That's twice in one day I've come close to losing my existence, and it's more than I can take. The shaking sets in first. It becomes so violent that my gown cocoon falls away on its own accord. My breathing comes in short bursts, never fully filling my lungs. Panic sets in with the realization that I'm not getting enough air.

My eyes dart around as the door to the cell slowly opens.

I freeze, knowing this will be my end. I can take no more.

"Michaela?" Penn whispers.

But I am paralyzed. I can't answer him. I can only watch him come into the cell, the girls trailing close behind him.

"Michaela," he says more urgently. It's still a whisper, but it sounds more like an impatient hiss this time. He doesn't see me yet, and his tone does nothing to spur me into movement. My friends walk further into the cell, letting the door close softly behind them. It's dark without the light from the hallway, but they're close enough to the window I can still see them, and if they turn around, they will see me.

Galenia is the one who notices me first. She rushes over and crouches down beside me. "Penn." It's nothing more than an echo of a whisper to me. I register the concern in her eyes, but I'm struggling to comprehend it. It's hard to care.

Penn kneels in front of me and takes my face in his hands, while Galenia puts a comforting arm around me.

"We thought you were gone," Penn whispers.

I can't answer him. Maybe I *am* gone. I've lost control of myself. It's as if I'm trapped in a frozen body.

Noticing how shaken I am, he wraps his arms around me, and Galenia tightens her half embrace. Horatia stands guard by the door, glancing nervously between the outside and us.

"Michaela, come back to me," Penn whispers in my ear. "I feel like I've already lost so much to this place. I can't lose *you* too. Come back to me." It doesn't help. I'm too far gone. And I'm starting to find comfort in this lack of being. I'm drifting. Their voices are too far away to reach me.

Galenia's expression turns grave, and she pushes Penn away from me. "Michaela. Remember the waterfalls on Earth." It's not a question; it's a command. "The mountains. The rolling hills and the white sand beaches. Remember the look on a child's face when you lead him or her into heaven."

Penn realizes what she's doing and cuts in. "Remember the man you told me about. How much he loved his wife despite their differences. How they sat on that bench after a fight, and each reached out to the other." It was something I'd shared with him when I brought him back to the heavens. I told him that story of hope after he asked me which of my experiences as a Reaper had moved me most. Although that couple's relationship wasn't perfect, far from it in fact, they never let go of hope, and so they always held on to each other.

Galenia smiled. "Remember the good." I notice her voice isn't echoing anymore. It's just above a whisper, but it's crystal clear.

The shaking slowly stops, and I take a deep breath and blink a few times, as if seeing my friends through new eyes. "We need to find Webber, free Kismet and the others, and get the heck out of here," I say. "I'm sick of this place."

"I couldn't agree more," Penn says, taking my arm and helping me up. I'm still a bit wobbly on my feet, but at least we're all here. At least we can move forward again.

Galenia holds onto one of my hands as we walk down the hallway, as if she's worried I'll succumb to panic again and be lost to them forever. I squeeze her hand, letting her know how much I appreciate her support.

The hallway ends and we are forced to choose, left or right. Or, more accurately, right or wrong. Or perhaps wrong or wrong if we're not even in the right part of hell. I have no idea where Webber could be at this point. So our choice is no more educated than if we were to flip a coin and let, well, *fate* decide.

"What do you think?" Penn asks.

It's then that I spot something lying off to the side of the hall. Curious, I release Galenia's hand and go to it. "It's a shoe," I declare. But not just any shoe. It's the black dress shoe of a male Reaper.

"Webber," I breathe, not wanting to scare away the hope that this single shoe has given me.

TWELVE

We follow the corridor until new doors appear. They're the same as the doors from the previous chambers—ancient splintered wood embedded with small, barred windows.

After glancing back and forth, searching for an errant demon, I glance inside the window of the first door. The man inside is surrounded by piles and piles of food—decadent sweets, luxurious cuts of steak, broiled lobsters, everything a foodie could possibly want. But he sits in a corner, crying as the food continues to appear in front of him. If he shifts by a matter of inches, more food piles up around him. The odor from the piles and piles of food pours out into the hall. The scents don't complement each other very well, so the stench makes me wrinkle my nose. Fresh-cooked fish and the sweet smell of homemade waffle cones. It must be overwhelming inside.

"Did that man have an eating disorder?" Galenia asks as she looks over my shoulder.

I shrug as we move to the next cell. This soul is surrounded by gorgeous women of all shapes, colors, and sizes. They're all demanding attention from him, but he's crying and trying to get away from them. They follow him when he retreats to the corner of the room, pawing at him as he goes. Some of them start taking off their clothes and brushing their bare skin against him.

It makes him run to another corner. But with only four corners in his room, the cycle quickly starts again.

"Was he a hermit? Why are there only women? I don't understand this area, Michaela. What's happening to these souls?" Galenia asks as we walk on to the next cell.

Penn turns sober. "I read about this when I was sneaking around as a Keeper. This is where people who lusted after others' things finally get what they wanted. But it doesn't make them happy, and it never will. The food isn't to their taste. Or those who have money in their cells…" He nods toward the next cell. The woman inside is sitting on a pile of gold—gold bars, goblets, plates, coins. The room looks like Scrooge McDuck's vault. But she's just sitting there with a dazed look on her face. "Gold is worthless in hell. She finally has what she wanted, what she lusted after her whole life, and now she can't do a single thing with it." I can hear the sadness in his voice as we keep walking.

The corridor is long, and there's a prisoner in each cell. As we near the end, I start to lose some of the excitement I felt upon finding that shoe. "If we don't find him, we need to consider what we want to do."

"You mean leave him here again?" Galenia asks, clearly opposed to the suggestion.

"We have to get out before the demons' workday starts, or we'll be trapped here right along with him."

Her frown tells me what she thinks of that, and Penn adds, "We're not leaving here without Kismet again."

"Penn, we may not have a choice. I'm not sure how long we've been in here. By the time we make our way back to the gate, we may be out of time."

Horatia, whose function as a Fate is, after all, to count off the days owed to each new soul, comes to my rescue. "We have time, Michaela. I will tell you when we need to go back. For now, we have time."

I nod. Although I don't fully understand how she can keep track of the passage of minutes and hours in hell, I trust her all the same.

"I found him," Galenia says as she stands outside a cell a

few doors up. The phrase cuts to my very core, and I'm torn between excitement and dread. What have they done to him?

We gather quickly around the window. The man inside the cell sits near a mound of wool. He's trying to make fabric or something out of it, but it's designed to be an impossible task. A spinning wheel sits off in the corner, but he can't seem to successfully get a handful of the wool. When he finally does, he pricks his finger on the needle several times while trying to get it onto the machine. He kicks the wheel over, throws the wool, spits on it, and then starts over, because he has nothing else to do. We watch him cycle through these actions several times, entranced by his torture.

Finally, he screams... and it snaps us all out of our trance.

"Webber," I whisper. "We're here for you."

THIRTEEN

They know who he is," Penn says as we stand outside the door watching him work the wool.

"No. They can't," I say. "Knowingly trapping a Reaper is one thing, but a Fate? They wouldn't cross that line." But even as the words leave my mouth, I know they're not true, no matter how badly I want to believe them. The demons do what they want inside these walls. As far as they're concerned, anyone stupid enough to wander into their lair deserves what they get.

This punishment—Webber working the wool, trying to make something—is clearly intended to mock him. But do they really know who he is, or are they simply trying to humiliate him to teach him the respect they think he needs?

We may never know the answer to that.

Tired of wondering, I pull the creaky door open and slip inside. The others follow close behind me, and they're careful to shut the door, giving us a small amount of privacy in case a demon should walk by.

"Webber," I say quietly, not wanting to startle him. But he ignores me. Or maybe he didn't hear.

I go closer to him and raise my voice a little. I don't want a demon to hear me shouting at him, but I need *him* to hear me. "Webber, come on. It's time to go." He ignores me again. We're only a few feet from each other, so this time, I know he had to hear me.

"What's happening?" Galenia quietly asks. At the sound of her voice, Webber flinches, but he refuses to look over at us. He simply continues his trek back and forth between the pile of wool and the wheel.

"Maybe he's not real," Penn says. "Maybe this is a trap for us." He looks around the dim room, as if readying himself for an attack.

Panic settles into my stomach, and I go back to the door, but it opens easily. "No. This isn't a trap for *us*," I say, watching Webber closely as he makes a few more trips from the pile of wool to the wheel.

I reach out and grab his shoulder. "Webber," I murmur.

"That's enough!" he cries out, slapping my hand away. "How much more do you need to torture me?" Tears stream freely down his cheeks now. He pushes past me so forcefully that I almost fall down.

Penn's eyes fill with anger as he helps me up. He looks about ready to punch Webber, and part of me wants to let him do it. Maybe it would snap him out of this. But no, that isn't my way.

I go over to him again. This time, I hold out my hand rather than touch him, hoping he'll come to me. Finally, he looks at me, *really* looks at me. The pain in his eyes is like nothing I've ever seen. It breaks my already broken heart into a thousand more pieces. But I still hold out my hand, a lifesaver in this sea of torture, if only he'll take it.

For a long time, we just stand there looking at each other. He looks tired. His bleach-blond hair that is normally perfectly combed to one side is incredibly disheveled. His dark gray eyes have lost their confidence. No longer do they hold any kind of challenge. The light has gone out of them.

After one day in hell, his clothes look like he's been wearing them for a week. The once form-fitting white shirt that fades to grey at the bottom is torn in several places and hangs off him, and his grey-to-black colored pants are dirty and covered in some kind of gray filth.

But I'm sure I don't look like the prettiest picture in the world after all we've been through. We've literally been to hell and back for him, and I'm sure he can see it on my face.

I hold steady, my hand extended to Webber, knowing he'll take it when he's ready.

After a little while longer, his face starts to soften, as if he's really starting to see me.

"What do you have to lose?" I ask.

He reaches out and takes my hand.

FOURTEEN

Before we can leave his cell, we have to come up with a plan. "I should've known it was you and not some cheap imitation. Your lack of an escape plan gives you away," Webber says with a hint of judgment in his voice, almost as if he's back to his old self.

"You're in a very precarious position to be so opinionated on the matter," Penn warns. Webber doesn't respond.

"I'll go on to the prison. The rest of you can get him out," Penn volunteers.

"You can't do that by yourself, Penn," I say. "Even if I gave you clear instructions on how to get there, you'd need someone else to help you free them. Honestly, I'm not sure what we should do. The last time I was there, I tried to break their chains and nothing worked. We'll need to work together."

Penn frowns, but I can tell he's relenting. "Fine. Horatia and Galenia, you can take Webber home. Michaela and I will go to the prison. If we're not back by the start of the workday, improvise. Webber can go back to work as the Spinner, and Michaela… well, maybe they won't notice she's gone with everything else that's going on."

I snort. "Right. And maybe the one who's responsible for all this will just bump into us on our way out and surrender."

He shrugs. "It could happen."

I know a shorter way out than the way we came in. But it involves going slightly deeper into hell, which the others aren't crazy about, particularly Webber.

"Look, once they discover you're gone, it's gonna be chaotic," I say. "We need to get you out as fast as possible. And wandering back through the chambers and caverns isn't ideal," I say.

Penn nods, although the other Fates look skeptical. "Fine. Lead the way."

I take them down to the end of the corridor, which opens to a pit of lava.

"Michaela, this is a dead end," Galenia points out, but her tone is more despondent than accusing.

Rather than respond, I point in the distance. There's a narrow stone bridge that traverses the lava.

"We'll be sitting ducks on that thing, Michaela," Penn says. "I think we should go back."

I frown. I'm convinced going back that way would be akin to suicide. I can already hear some scrambling echoing down the corridor behind us. "We can't go back by Webber's cell. It'll be crawling with demons very soon, if it isn't already. They've never had a successful break out before, and there are reasons for that. The Hunters are good at what they do, and they'll be after us before long. We need a quick getaway. The outskirts of hell are just on the other side of this bridge. If we can make it, we're home free."

Horatia swallows hard. "*If* we can make it," she chokes out.

"We knew this wouldn't be easy. This is the way out. I promise," I say, imploring them to make haste. "The longer we stand here and debate it, the greater the danger of being caught. We don't know what they'll do to us if we're caught, but *not* knowing might be the worst torture of all."

Webber laughs darkly at that. A maniacal look spreads across his face as he says, "You have no idea."

Galenia is the first one to take a step forward. "You've gotten us this far," she says as she walks toward the bridge without looking back. Webber needs some encouraging, so Penn jerks him along. His resistance ends when a roar splits the air. It's easy to guess what's happened—his empty cell has been discovered.

We skirt the narrow ledge that runs along the edge of the pool and leads to the bridge. It's tricky in a few places, with fallen boulders to go around and cracks to jump over. I watch my footing carefully, but Webber isn't so surefooted, nor is he watching where he's going. He's too busy looking over his shoulder with wild eyes.

It's not surprising when Webber loses his balance and grabs the closest person, who happens to be Horatia. She goes over the edge, but not before Penn leaps forward and grabs her arm. Webber hangs from the hem of her dress, and I can hear it tearing.

"Webber, grab my leg. It won't hold," she begs, referring to her dress.

"Stop kicking," he yells, the desperation in his voice echoing off the cavern walls.

"Quiet… both of you," I whisper, worried this slip up will draw attention to us.

"Oh, I'm sorry. Are you dangling above a pool of lava?" Webber snaps.

"No, but that's because I was watching where I was going," I say, and I immediately clap my hand over my mouth. "I'm sorry, Webber, I don't know where that came from." But I do. This journey is grating on me, and his attitude isn't helping. We've stuck our necks out an awful long way for him, particularly since he hasn't even thanked us.

A very dark thought creeps into my head just then. If he fell, we could easily pull Horatia up and move on.

Just as soon as I think it, I chide myself. I've been in hell too long; it's starting to affect me. We need to get out of here, and we need to get out *now*.

Meanwhile, Penn is sweating bullets, struggling to hold them both as he lies on his stomach, hanging halfway over the ledge. "I'd love to hear the rest of this terribly interesting conversation, but I'd appreciate it if you'd all shut up and give me a hand."

Galenia and I rush to his aid; I lay flat on the thin ledge, letting a small part of my body hang over, while Galenia crouches behind me and holds on to my legs. Once I'm in position, I grab Horatia's arm. With more leverage, Penn and I are able to pull Horatia up, but she can't clamber onto the ledge because Webber is weighing her down. Penn tries to get Webber to grab the ledge and let go of Horatia, but he can't get their movements coordinated. Webber is thrashing around, trying to get purchase on the wall with his foot, but it's not helping, and it's making it hard to keep my grip on Horatia.

"Webber, you fool. You're going to kill us both," Horatia shouts at him. I cringe as their voices echo off the stone walls around us. Hopefully, the demons are making too much of a commotion to hear us. But I know it's only a matter of time before the Hunters are set loose, and we're not exactly keeping a low profile.

"Come on, let's pull them up together," I tell Penn. We tug Horatia's arms with all our might, and I can only imagine that with Webber pulling her down and us pulling her up, she must feel like she's being torn apart. She bites down on her bottom lip, and I appreciate her effort to keep the noise down.

Penn grunts as we heft Horatia halfway onto the ledge. Her entire upper body is safe, but Webber is still dangling. I hold her in place while Penn reaches over and tries to retrieve Webber. Despite the fact that Webber is panicking, Penn grabs hold of his shirt with one hand and his arm with the other, and muscles him onto the ledge.

There's a moment where he's free of Horatia, and I'm not sure Penn will get him up onto the ledge we're all so precariously piled up on, so I squeeze my eyes shut and hope for the best while I hold on for dear life to Horatia.

When I'm finally brave enough to open my eyes again, I see Webber in a heap against the wall, and Penn looking like he's about to beat the living daylights out of him. "Penn. Not now. Help me with Horatia," I warn.

"This isn't over," he says, his voice low and menacing, matching the terrifying tone of our surroundings. I'm starting to worry about Penn. He's not himself. This place has sunk its claws in him—it's affecting him more than it is the rest of us, and I can only imagine it has something to do with his affinity toward humanity. I can hardly fault him for that.

But to my relief, Penn leaves Webber panting in a heap by the wall and comes to my rescue. Working together, it's easy for Penn and me to hoist Horatia up onto the ledge. We hug her when she's safely on the closest thing to solid ground we have at the moment.

Penn goes back to Webber. "That's twice you've nearly killed us all. If you think for a second I was on board with coming back here and saving you, you're wrong. Next time you pull something like that, it will be your last. Mark my words, Webber."

We all spend a tense moment shifting our weight on the edge of a pit of lava, waiting to see if Webber will respond.

When he doesn't say anything, Horatia speaks up. "Who's for Webber walking in front from now on?"

We all look back at him, still lying on his side up against the wall, staring into the lava pit with terrified eyes.

It's in that moment that I'm reminded of our larger purpose… and the fact that we're losing our chance at achieving it the longer we delay. "Webber, either you make your way to the front, or we move on without you," I say, hating myself for saying it, hating him for putting me in such a terrible position.

He looks up at me with that lost, wild look in his eyes. "You wouldn't dare," he says, but he's scared, not defiant.

"Don't force my hand," I say, standing up straight. He slowly stands, and we press ourselves against the wall, making it easier for him to climb over us.

First, he must get past Penn. It's a tense moment for all of us. I fear he will throw Webber into the pit, and frankly, I wouldn't entirely blame him for it. But though Penn glares at Webber in hatred and balls his hands in fists, he allows Webber to stumble past him without hitting him. The rest of us try not to touch him either, and we certainly don't let him grab onto us as he makes his clumsy way to the front. I, for one, don't want a repeat of what just happened. I've always known him to be a bit of a weasel, but I've lost what little trust I had for him. So when he tries to grab my hand for balance, I twist away.

"No. Don't touch me," I coldly say. Hell is getting to me too. I think it's getting to all of us.

Once he's at the front, I position myself behind him. The three other Fates, with Penn in the rear, follow. Finally, we make it to the base of the bridge.

"We will be very exposed on the bridge. It's important that we get across as quickly as possible."

The bridge is nothing more than a stone walkway. No rails, no ledges, nothing to protect us from falling into the lava. Our only lucky break is that it's wider than the ledge we just walked across. Two of us could walk shoulder to shoulder without any problem, although it's safer to walk one by one.

I push Webber out onto the walkway first, following close behind. "Run," I command.

But as soon as we step on to the bridge, fire rains down on us from above. "It's a trap. Go!" I urge, but Webber is frozen in place. "You'll get burned if you stay here. Go!" I yell, pushing him more forcefully.

Finally, he starts to put one foot in front of another, but not before a fiery piece of ash falls in my hair, setting it alight. Galenia beats at it furiously, putting out the flames with her bare hands.

"We have to get out of here," she yells above the roar of rushing fire all around us.

"I couldn't agree more," I say, pushing Webber along, urging him to pick up the pace. Finally, an ember lands on his shoulder, burning through his clothing and contacting his skin.

He cries out in pain, and then flat-out runs toward the other end of the bridge. We breach the halfway point, and we're far enough for me to see the opening to the corridor that leads to the outskirts of hell. We're so close...

Then I hear an ominous voice from behind me.

"Reaper," it calls, and I screech to a halt. It's as if my feet obey his commands rather than my own. The others crash into me, but Webber keeps running on ahead. That's for the best.

"Go," I command the others. "Go. I will handle this. I'll be right behind you," I promise, and they reluctantly step around me. Penn is the last to move past me, and he squeezes my hand in passing.

"Michaela," he says, but I silence him. I don't know if this is goodbye. If so, I don't have time to process that. I only know that I need to save them so they can save Kismet and the others. And I can give them the time to do that.

"Go! I'll meet you at the gate." Penn frowns and reluctantly follows the others.

The hunter is at least three times my size. Fiery light shines through the cracks in his black skin and waves of heat pour from his eyes and mouth. Black horns curve around his face, connecting with a line of fire. He holds a stone ax of some kind, though I'm not well versed enough in demon weaponry to identify it. All I know is it's bigger than my body, rectangular and worse than deadly. With it, I know he can erase me from this world. He growls at me and the sound blends with the fire roaring all around me, amplifying the racket.

"What do you think you're doing?" he snarls. I can physically feel the heat from his words, and it blows my hair back around me, making me stand up a little straighter.

"The right thing," I say. I'm scrambling for ideas as he steps out onto the bridge. I can't just stall him and expect to survive. I have to either stop him or get him to go in another direction without me. But how?

That's when it occurs to me. The souls. Will they protect me here in hell? The ghosts tried to hurt me, but they owe nothing to anyone here in hell. But it feels like it's worth a shot now that I'm standing in front of the Hunter. *Anything* is worth a shot at this point.

I raise my arms as the Hunter's fierce growl sends ripples through my dress and warms my face.

"Souls of hell. You are needed. Come to me now," I say as calmly as possible, looking up toward my raised arms. When nothing happens, I start to feel foolish.

The Hunter laughs—a terrible sound that makes rocks fall

from the walls and crash into the lava below. It splashes up onto the bridge, taking chunks of the structure along with it as it seeps back into the depths. "You're a fool. The souls of hell know there's no redemption for them. You are alone, Reaper." I turn to look behind me, and he's right. My friends are gone. I breathe a sigh of relief. Hopefully, they're safe, for now.

Continuing to hold my hands up above my head, I say again, louder this time, "Souls of hell. You are needed. Come to me now!" I clap my hands together, making a sound like thunder. The Hunter stops advancing on me as a ball of light appears between my raised hands. A soul appears out of nowhere in front of me. Wordlessly, he turns to face the Hunter. Suddenly, there are more and more souls, until there is a wall of them separating me from the Hunter.

There is an angry roar that shakes the very foundation of hell, but I don't feel the heat from it. The souls are completely blocking him from me. The bridge starts to collapse under the Hunter's rage, and the souls start chanting.

"Go." They say the single word over and over again, as if they are one soul, not thousands. It's a haunting and sad sound, making it difficult for me to leave them. But I know what I must do. This will probably be the end of them, but at least they will have redeemed themselves by helping another soul.

The Hunter is breathing fire at them, melting them out of existence one by one. They're advancing on him, trying to overwhelm him. I honestly can't tell who will win. Part of me wants to stay and watch, but their relentless chanting finally spurs me into movement.

"Thank you," I say before I turn and run.

I find myself alone on the outskirts of hell. Demons are rushing everywhere, but none of them seem to take notice of me. I can only hope it stays that way. Sneaking from one hiding place to the next, I make my way toward the gate, looking for any sign of my friends.

Finally, I emerge from the darkness and see the four of

them huddling near the gate. Horatia and Galenia are hugging Penn while Webber stands alone off to the side.

As I make my way toward them, I spot an errant demon out of the corner of my eye. He's rushing at them with wild eyes. Webber sees him first and runs out of the gate without looking back. Galenia sees him next, but she can't do anything because she's mid-hug with Penn. Stepping out in front of them, Horatia holds out her hands to stop him.

"Stop, demon," I say authoritatively. I must still be running on adrenaline from my encounter with the Hunter, because I sure don't feel as powerful as I sound.

He screeches to a halt, close enough to touch Horatia. Her lip is curled against the scent of his rotting flesh, but she doesn't move even an inch.

"How dare you attempt to lay hands on a Reaper," I say, surprising myself by how confident I sound. "We're just finishing a tour. It shouldn't surprise you that we would seek to comfort each other after seeing the horrors in your home," I say, shocked by how easily the lies roll off my tongue. I shouldn't be able to lie. Heavenly beings can't do it. Perhaps the rules are different here in hell. Or perhaps I've lost a part of myself to the darkness. I don't get much time to dwell on it before the demon is firing back at me.

"That's a lie and you know it, Reaper," he snarls at me. I resist the urge to cringe away from him.

"Do not try to manipulate me. You're wasting my precious time. Be gone," I command.

He hesitates, and it's enough for me to realize that I can win this fight. He backs up automatically as I take several steps toward him. "Don't make me tell you again," I insist.

"But there's been an escape. I'm afraid I must keep you here." Although his voice is still shrill, it's lost its menacing quality. It's now disgustingly humble. Almost sniveling. Almost apologetic.

"Demons do not command me," I say, advancing on him further, totally unsure of what I will do if he stops backing up and I actually reach him.

"But… my superiors. We've been instructed not to let anyone come or go."

"That is not my concern. It seems to me you have a serious management problem here in hell. I'm sure *my* superior will be *very* interested to hear that." I stand straight and firm, challenging him to test me.

"No. Please. Just go. I'll say there was no one here. Just go," he says, continuing to back up.

"You first," I say. He does a strange little half bow, revealing his tiny, black wings, and turns to run back the way he came.

The group collectively exhales, and they rush over to me, all of them speaking at once as they hug me and clap me on the back.

Finally, Penn's voice breaks through. "How did you escape?"

"That's a story for another time," I say, looking at the other Fates. "Go. You must get Webber home. Penn and I will meet up with you as soon as we can."

Horatia hesitates. "As far as I'm concerned, Webber can take care of himself. I want to stay with you."

Galenia glances at us, and then over her shoulder toward the gate.

Penn wraps his arms around their shoulders. "I want you to go home. I don't want to worry about you in the depths of hell anymore. There are demons swarming everywhere. Go home— make sure Webber is okay. And cover for us if we take too long. I need you in heaven now. I promise that we'll see you again soon."

The girls hold back tears as the three Fates embrace. I dab the moisture away from my own eyes and glance around, checking for more wandering demons.

"I don't want to rush you, but you should go if you're going to leave. We can't linger here any longer," I say.

Galenia and Horatia look at me and make their approach. "Thank you, Michaela," Galenia says. "We both knew you were an amazing soul, but this journey has shown us just how much. You're like a sister to us. Be sure and come back."

"You have some precious cargo with you," Horatia says as

she nods at Penn. He smiles in return. "You don't have much time left, half the night is gone. So please hurry home."

My only response is to hug them both. "Good luck," I say as they walk back through the gate, leaving Penn and me alone in hell.

FIFTEEN

By the time we make our way back into the outskirts of hell, the demons are crawling everywhere. There's no way we're going to get to the prison without being seen.

We backtrack, debating what to do. There's only one way in and out of the prison, but there are a few different paths leading to it. We hide in the shadows of a large rock as a demon rushes past us, moving too fast to notice.

"We're close to a tunnel that might get us there," I whisper, thinking out loud.

"How?" Penn asks, looking around at the stone walls that loom all around us.

"It's deeper underground. It's almost like a sewer drain on Earth. But it's not for sewage. To be honest, I don't know why it's there."

Penn looks at me, a wary expression on his face. "Where does the sewer drain lead?"

"I think it pops out near the entrance to the prison. If I'm remembering correctly. It's been a while since I studied the maps during my training, but I remember seeing a grate near the prison door."

"This from the Reaper who got us lost trying to find Webber," he says, needling me.

"You got any better ideas, hotshot?" I ask, grateful to have him with me to keep my mood light.

"No, but I wish I did. I'd rather not trudge through some unknown sewer in the depths of hell. But hey, since we're already here, why not?" he adds with a smirk.

I smile back and nod. "Let's go." The opening to the tunnel is down the corridor and around a few turns. We have to do some fancy maneuvering to avoid being seen, and I know if we don't get below deck, we'll be discovered sooner rather than later.

Finally, we're within striking range of the opening. We wait for a lull in the flow of demons and then dart over to it. I crouch down to open the iron grate on the floor. It's not as heavy as I anticipated, and it jolts open and nearly bounces back down before I manage to catch it.

The darkness under it is all consuming, but we'll have to worry about light later.

Or not. Penn grabs a torch off the wall while I frantically try to prop open the grate. I take one last look left and right before slipping down into the darkness. He follows me and pulls the grate down behind him. I can only hope that the clang is obscured by the commotion of the demons as they rush around, searching for the escaped soul.

I push Penn away from the opening in the low ceiling as a pair of demons passes over the top of us. Thankfully, they're too absorbed in their task to notice us.

"Did you hear about the Hunter?" one says. Its jagged voice echoes slightly in the tunnel.

"Yes. This is obviously not an average soul that's escaped."

"It wasn't a soul that eliminated the Hunter."

Eliminated? I think. So the ghosts overcame him. I smile to myself, feeling pride in those lost souls who came to my rescue.

"Like I said, this isn't an average soul. Obviously, the Reapers want him for something."

"I heard he *was* a Reaper."

"What? No. That can't be right. A Reaper would never be trapped down here. Maybe it's just a soul one of the Reapers misplaced. But once a soul's in here, he belongs to us."

They're walking away, so the response is hard to make out, but I do hear the last part. "They'll all pay for their mistake."

The dark promise is enough to give me a chill in this hot, fiery place. But we're committed to our cause now, so Penn and I just exchange a look and start walking toward the prison.

Our footsteps seem to echo off the close walls, and we walk slowly, cautiously, through the darkness to try to lessen the sound. The red glow is disconcerting, and we can't see more than a few feet in front of us. We don't speak as we follow the tunnel.

Unexpectedly, it forks off, and we're forced to make a decision about where we need to go. Rather than guess, I backtrack to the last place we spotted a grate. Penn agrees to hoist me up so I can get an idea of where we are.

After resting the red torch against the wall, he makes a cradle for my foot with his hand. Just as he hoists me over his head, I spot huge, glowing red eyes in the distance behind him, down the center fork.

"Penn," I whisper, fear making my voice ragged.

"What?"

I hastily climb down and point. He turns, grabs the torch and my hand, and we run full speed down the left fork. There is no sound of the creature. No wind from its breath. *Nothing.* So I chance a glance over my shoulder. Those glowing eyes are the same distance from us as they were before. They're definitely following us.

"The eyes of hell. They'll know we're here. We have to blind them," I say.

"The eyes of hell? I didn't see anything about that in the Keeper's literature."

"Must've missed that section. They help the Hunters find any escapees. They're stationed at intervals throughout hell, and they record what they see for the demons. Apparently, we found one."

"Great," he says as we run. "How do we blind it?"

There is so much fire in hell—the eyes themselves resemble

twin flames—so the answer seems inevitable. "We need water."

We pass under another grate, and the demons are scrambling above our heads. "They're in the tunnels," I hear one of them shout.

"The tears of the damned," I say, barely above a whisper, fearing the words even as I say them. I know all too well what I'm calling down on us.

The tears are a last-resort weapon created for the Reapers, although I'm sure they've never been used before. We all know how to execute them in theory. If a Reaper gets into big trouble in hell, and this certainly qualifies, the tears can be summoned one time, and one time only, to extinguish all nearby flames. The flames that live within the demons are also susceptible to the tears, which is why they are such a dangerous weapon. But I have trouble sympathizing with the demons that are currently hunting us.

The tears are a sign that we are never alone or forgotten. Even in the depths of hell.

As soon as the words are out of my mouth, I hear the roaring.

"What did you do?" Penn asks.

"I may have just drowned us in an effort to save us."

"Can we drown?" Penn asks. I honestly don't know, but I'm not willing to risk it. As the water comes rushing toward us, we both instinctively run. I see a small crevice in the wall and duck into it, pulling Penn in beside me. With any luck, the speed of the water rushing by us will be enough to keep us safe from it. The space is just wide enough for us to wedge into it sideways. Even my head is turned, so I can watch the wall of water pass us. It would be strangely beautiful if the sound wasn't so terrifying, and I didn't know that the water had been borne of the suffering in hell.

As the water slows down, I start to worry this will be our doom. It seeps into our crevice quickly, but it never gets very deep. Most of it has washed away.

But our gratitude is temporary. Demons drop down from the grate nearest us and begin to search the tunnel.

"Find them," a deep voice says, and we hear several sets of footsteps going off in all directions.

Penn's torch is gone, lost to the wave of water. We don't speak to each other, for fear of drawing attention to ourselves. All we can do is wait.

It seems like an eternity in the tunnel, but it probably isn't more than a few moments. We're both anxious to move on, collect the souls, and get the hell out of hell.

The demons finally split up to search for us, but they leave one behind to patrol the tunnel, and he takes the torch with him.

At first, he stays close to us—pacing back and forth, looking all over—but we pull back into the crevice until we're crammed shoulder to shoulder, as far out of sight as possible.

To my relief, the demon finally wanders far enough down the tunnel that we can sneak out of our spot and continue down the path. The demon's not trying to be quiet as he paces back and forth, splashing in the puddles left behind by the tears, and his sounds cover ours as we sneak out of our safe haven. We take deliberate steps, as fast as we can go, but we're not flat-out running. The last thing we want to do is attract the notice of any more demons.

Without the light of the torch, our progress forward is difficult. We stick to the walls, feeling our way along. But I have no idea where we are at this point. In our frantic dash to get away from the wall of water, I lost track of our position. I need to get out and reassess.

Penn realizes the same thing, and we stop wordlessly below the next grate we reach. We both know this could be suicide. The second I pop my head up, anyone who's in the corridor will see me. But I can think of no other or better solution. We can't wander the dark tunnel forever. Eventually, we have to go topside. Now's as good a time as any, I suppose.

Penn cradles his hands for me yet again. Before I put my foot into them, I look over his shoulder for the eyes that started this whole misstep. But there's nothing but darkness all around us. The only light comes from the grate.

He hoists me up carefully, so as not to hit my head on the grate. Before I push it open, I take a moment to listen for any noise. It's oddly quiet. I strain to see something through the grate, but the only thing I can see well is the ceiling above the grate.

I carefully push the grate open enough to peer out. It's an empty hallway. I'm relieved, but at the same time, I was hoping for some markings, something to give an indication of where we are. As I shove the grate all the way open, Penn launches me through it.

Now we're faced with a different problem. How am I going to get Penn out? Demons all have wings and can fly in and out of places like this, so there's no easy way out. The grate is too small to use as a ladder. If I lay flat, he can reach up and grab my arms, but I don't think I'm strong enough to pull him out.

An idea suddenly occurs to me, and I grab the grate and drag it away from the hole. Then I stretch out on my stomach and muscle the grate over my legs, hoping the added weight will be enough to anchor the two of us. The grate is pressing down on my legs hard, cutting off circulation to my feet, but this just might work.

I reach down into the hole, praying no demons come across us in such a vulnerable situation.

"But," Penn protests.

"I don't have any better ideas. Just try it. If you pull me in there with you, we'll try something else."

Nodding, he hesitantly reaches for me. He just barely manages to reach the tips of my fingers, so he jumps up a little to give himself some leverage. It works great until he comes back down and jerks hard on my hands.

I slip toward him, but the grate digs my knees into the stone, ripping my dress as it goes. It holds, and I don't go over. I bite my lip to prevent myself from screaming out in pain.

"Sorry," he sheepishly says.

"Just get out of that hole." I say through gritted teeth.

Penn tries to swing himself up, but the hole isn't big enough for him to get a grip with his feet on the other side. Instead, he ends up hitting the top of the tunnel with his butt.

"Nice payback," he says, grimacing.

I can't help but smile through my pain. My arms and legs are on fire, and my knees feel like they've been through a meat grinder. I'm ready to move on, but he's still hanging from my hands, no further along than he was before.

Finally, he transfers all his weight to one of my arms. "You're going to dislocate my arm," I say through gritted teeth.

"Not if I can do this quickly."

Grabbing at him with my free hand, I try to relieve some of the weight. I don't really succeed, but it feels better to be doing something. He climbs up my arm hand over hand, like I'm some kind of rope. When he gets to my shoulder, he grabs the edge of the hole and hoists himself out, relieving me entirely of his weight. He settles down on his back next to my legs and pushes the heavy grate off me. I roll toward him, so we're both staring up at the stone ceiling.

"Awfully quiet back here. Where are we?"

I drape my arm over my eyes. "I don't know. Right now, I really don't care." I'm visualizing that peaceful garden God took me to. I would do almost anything to be back there. But then I think about God's ocean of tears, and I remember what I'm doing in hell in the first place.

Sighing, I sit up and assess the damage to my knees. Blood seeps out of the road burn left by the stone floor. Blowing on them, I try to relieve some of the stinging. I pull my dress away from them, hoping it doesn't dry to the blood and stick. Something from the corner of my eye captures my attention as I do this, something that reminds me of who stands with us.

This isn't just any unmarked, unoccupied corridor of hell.

Penn follows my gaze. "The prison."

SIXTEEN

The door is barely perceptible, save for the symbol carved into the stone and a light outline. Though we still have the hardest part of our mission ahead of us—getting those poor captured souls out—I know beyond a shadow of a doubt we're in the right place, and it feels like a win.

"How did you get inside?" Penn asks.

I shrug. "It wasn't locked when I was here. I just pushed the door open."

Penn hesitantly holds his hand out to the door as I scan the area for demons. When I look back, he's still holding his hand just shy of the stone.

"What are you waiting for?" I whisper.

"What's beyond this door is my personal hell. I know that. Seeing the suffering of Kismet and Andrew and the other souls I've spun. I… I intended so much more for them. Once I open this door, it'll all become real… Frankly, now that I'm here, I don't really want to go inside."

I put my hand on his shoulder. "Neither do I, and I've already seen what's in there." I'm not sure my sentiment counts as encouragement, but he puts his hand on the door nevertheless. Despite the appearance of the heavy stone, it pushes inward without resistance.

He's right. What's inside is horrible. Pure souls, ones that don't belong in hell, are chained to the walls, crying and moaning. Some are not moving at all.

I carefully push the stone most of the way back into its original position. I don't know if it's possible to seal us inside, so I can't bring myself to close it completely, but I also don't want to make it obvious we're in here.

When I turn around, I witness the moment Penn sees Kismet. Her hair is a knotted mess, and her bright green eyes have lost their sparkle. She was most beautiful, shining thread he ever created. Even I could spot her brilliance among the millions of threads in the tapestry. She just stood out. But now her sparkle is gone, and she's literally wasting away.

"Kismet," he breathes out as he falls to the floor at her side. She barely sees him. She's looking at Andrew, who is much worse off than she is. Her true love, made by Penn to complement her perfectly in every way, is already becoming transparent in places. He literally looks ghoulish.

After a quick scan of the room, I notice one soul is missing. "Nysa. Where is Nysa?"

Andrew picks up his head at the sound of my voice. But his gaze lands on Penn, not me. His once blue eyes have taken on a sickly gray tone. There's no spark in them anymore, and his gaze sends a chill down my spine.

"Penn, is that you?" Andrew weakly says. "It's good to see you."

Penn manages a genuine smile and claps his hand on his friend's shoulder. I wince, not sure if it will pass through or not, but by some miracle, Penn's hand lands firmly on Andrew's spirit.

"This wasn't how I envisioned our next meeting."

Andrew scoffs, which ends up sounding like nothing more than a short exhale of breath. It's almost imperceptible, but there's a half smile on his face. "Yes, well, you always were getting me into trouble."

"Hey now, this isn't my fault."

Kismet interrupts their banter. "Penn. You have to help

him."

She looks at him with her faded green eyes, a shadow of their former beauty, and I can see his heart breaking before me. But he smiles at her anyway.

"That's why we're here."

I hate to interrupt their reunion, but we need to get out of here. "Nysa, Andrew. Where is Nysa?" I ask again.

"She faded away." His voice is no more than a whisper. I know he's not far behind her. But as I assess the others, I realize there are a few worse off than him.

"She faded away?" Penn asks, clearly not accepting this is even a possibility for the souls inside. That would mean failure.

As his message sinks in, my legs go out from under me, and I collapse near Andrew. "She ceased to exist," I whisper, as if saying it quietly won't make it true.

"She *what?*" Penn looks to me for an explanation, comfort, something.

But I'm afraid I will fall short. "Extinction is a kind of release for a soul who belongs in hell. It's an escape from the eternal torture. But souls who are heaven bound should never face extinction. It's the worst possible outcome. It's what will happen to you if you're discovered," I say to Penn.

He swallows and turns back to face Kismet. "I won't let that happen to you." But she still doesn't look at him. He turns to look at the other sad souls chained to the prison. "Any of you."

Nysa spent the most time in the prison. Perhaps that's why she was the first to dissipate. "Who did this to you?" I ask, hoping one of them will have an answer. "Who brought you here?"

Andrew is the one who speaks. "I didn't recognize her. Nysa seemed to know her, when she was still coherent."

"So it's the same person? And she's a woman? She's not working with anyone else?"

"From what we've been able to piece together…" He pauses and takes a deep breath, shifting his weight as if he's terribly uncomfortable. Of course, he must be. A human year has passed while he's in this position—arms chained above his head, a hard stone floor underneath him. He coughs a little before continuing. "She started out on her own, but she's gained an accomplice. Someone like you, I think. He's the one who brought me here. He was dressed just like you, Penn. Black and white." He gestured with his head to Penn's uniform.

The missing Reaper. It has to be him. But is he helping her willingly? Still, we need to get them out. *Now.* That's a question for another day.

"What else do you know about this woman?" I ask, digging for clues that will help us find and stop her.

"Like I said, Nysa seemed to know her. Said she'd met her at work. But the rest of us didn't recognize her. I'm not sure Kismet even saw her."

Kismet shakes her head. "Just the one like you," she chokes out. "He promised to take me to the right place after you left me at the gate of heaven, and I trusted him."

The last phrase cuts me to the bone.

"I'm sorry," I say to her, hoping she knows how deeply I mean it. But her soul seems incapable of receiving apologies just now. She's returned to staring at Andrew, concern rolling off her like fog off a lake.

And then something Andrew said makes me pause. "Nysa knew her from work?" I ask, but don't wait for an answer. "Is she human?"

"I assumed she was," Andrew says, almost phrasing it like a question. He clearly knows Penn and I are different…and he knows the one who brought them here is different, but I'm not sure he comprehends what it means.

I lean back against the wall next to Andrew. *Human.* It's not something I ever considered. How can it be true? Humans don't know about our world—let alone how to navigate it. One of us must be responsible…

But if it's true… It means a human has breeched our world in every way possible. It means she knows about the tapestry, and she's learned how to cut threads. It means she's either kidnapped or somehow gained alliance with a Reaper, and then reopened the prison of souls to keep her victims. These seem like herculean tasks for a simple human. There has to be more to her than that.

"A name. Do you have a name?" I ask, but Andrew is done talking to me. His breathing is labored, and he's hanging his head more and more. I look at Penn, concerned, but he's watching Kismet.

"Mara," she says in a small voice. "Nysa repeated it often."

"Penn? Is she really human?" I ask.

Penn scratches his head. "I don't know. I need to think about it. I didn't make her recently, that's for sure."

"Was she an old woman?" I ask the room.

"Middle aged, older than any of us," a soul against the opposite wall answers. He's even thinner than Andrew is, and I'm surprised he can speak at all.

After a few beats of silence, Kismet finally looks up at Penn. "Have you come to save us?"

"Yes," he says without hesitation.

But before he can free her, I hear a couple of demons approaching just outside the door.

I motion for Penn to position himself as a prisoner, and I stand beside him. Both of us take care not to lock the shackles we're pretending to use.

The demon pushes the door open so hard it slams against the back wall, making a thunderous sound. Standing as still as possible, I say a silent prayer of thanks that no one was imprisoned behind the door. With any luck, he won't look closely at my Reaper clothes—or Penn's, for that matter. To be honest, after all our travels, my dress is torn to bits, and the colors are so dulled by dirt and dust, a cursory glance may not reveal us as Reapers.

Hope is my only companion as the demon lingers in the room. From the way he's looking back and forth, it's clear he's searching for someone, but whether it's Penn, me, Webber, or the other Fates, I can't be sure. Maybe all of the above.

Penn has strategically positioned himself between two souls, using them to hide most of his body from the doorway. The demon would have to walk right in front of him to see what he's wearing or see his face.

I'm all alone on my side of the prison, but before the demon opened the door, I tucked the skirt of my dress behind me, making it appear shorter, masking the distinctive coloring. I hang my head, only peeking out occasionally.

After what feels like an eternity, the demon snorts and moves on, pulling the door closed behind him. As it slams shut, I breathe out a sigh of relief.

"We need to get out of here. *Now*," I say. But it suddenly occurs to me that most of them probably can't walk. In fact, I think Kismet is the only one who'd be capable of it at this point. Maybe one other soul. But that leaves four of them for us to carry out of hell, including Andrew.

I look at Penn, whose stricken expression tells me that he's reached the same conclusion.

"What do you want to do?" he asks.

"I'm not sure. I don't think we can get them all." Suddenly, I regret suggesting that the other Fates leave with Webber. If we had them, we could probably manage. Probably.

Of course, there's also the problem of how we'll get them free of their restraints and out of this place. I make my way to the soul who seems the worst off. He's so transparent, it seems like I could put my hand straight through him.

He must be Jeff, the second soul who was taken. He's hanging limply, barely conscious. He's so thin that I wonder how the shackles are even holding him up.

The keyhole on his shackles is small. His bindings are iron, so I search the room for a small iron key.

"Penn, we need a key," I say. He's already fiddling with Kismet's shackles, trying to release them.

Kismet's expression is forlorn. "It's hanging next to the door."

Whirling around, I easily spot the tiny object hanging from a hook just to the left of the now-closed door. The way this woman has tortured these souls turns my stomach—so much so that I need to hold it with my hand for a moment as I retrieve the key.

I curse myself for not seeing it the last time I was here. It's small and unobtrusive, just above my own eye level. I have to reach up to get it. But still, if I'd seen it then, I could've saved Nysa. Maybe. Probably. I debate the possibilities in my mind as I take the key back to Jeff, who's barely visible by the time I crouch down in front of him.

The key gets stuck in his lock almost as soon as I put it in. The iron is old, and the two don't fit together as they once did. But after some jimmying, I feel it click, and the lock springs open. I pull it out and swing the bar off his wrists.

His arms fall lifelessly to his sides, and he looks up at me for a quick moment before he fades away right before my eyes.

I feel like melting away with him. I've let another one slip through my fingers. The despair threatens to crush me as I sit back in front of the empty space the soul occupied moments before.

"Michaela, we need to save the ones we can," Penn says, trying to bring me out of my despair.

But in that moment, I'm too horrified to move.

"I'm sorry," I whisper to the emptiness in front of me.

An alarm sounds before I can finish the sentence. It pierces my ears, and both Penn and I double over and cover our ears. The shrieking makes it difficult to think.

I immediately know what it means. And judging from the look on Penn's face, he does too. I imagine my own expression mirrors the terror he's feeling. We say in unison, "The Cleanse," although I can't hear him over the shrieking.

It must have been triggered when I unlocked the first prisoner's shackles. And now, we're sitting ducks. The Cleanse eliminates all intruders. It's fast moving, and nearly impossible to escape. There are no first-hand reports of how it works, since no one has ever survived it, but I have a pretty good idea that it's not something I want to witness. It has only been used two, maybe three, times in recorded memory. It's a last-resort weapon, used only when the demons are most desperate to regain control of their home.

"Penn, we need to go. *Now.*" He's too busy fumbling with Kismet's shackles to listen, but I have the key. His plight is fruitless.

Quickly, I move on to the next prisoner, unlock her shackles with record speed, move to the next, and then toss the key to Penn so he can free the most tattered souls from the other side of the prison. The key clangs to the ground as I start hoisting the souls onto my shoulders. They're not heavy, but it will still be a burden to carry them through hell fast enough to escape the Cleanse.

As we free them, the souls seem to breathe a sigh of relief, as if simply releasing them eases their torture. One even manages a half smile.

"Penn!" I yell. He grabs the key and starts to work on Kismet. "Not her! Get one of the others. We'll come back for her."

The look he gives me tells me how much I've crushed him, but I'm not kidding. "Save someone from extinction, Penn. She isn't even close. She'll be safe here."

"No, you can't leave us here," Kismet pleads, breaking my heart even more.

As the fire roaring outside becomes so loud I can barely hear his words, Andrew summons energy from somewhere and calms her. He is exactly what she needs, even now. "Kismet, we will be fine. They won't leave us here. Our time here is limited now. Take strength from that. They will die if they stay here for us," he soothes as huge tears pool in her dull, green eyes.

Penn nods to his friend, a silent thank you, reluctantly snatching up the key and unlocking a soul a few spots down from Andrew. The key clangs to the ground.

In that moment, I almost think we could take them. We worked so quickly, maybe we could do it. Then, I see the orange glow forming around the outer edge of the door.

Anxiously, I adjust the souls on my shoulder. "We need to go. Now," I shout above the flames licking at the door of the prison.

It's torture to leave Andrew and Kismet behind, but we have no choice. The Cleanse is coming for us. Penn takes one of my souls to lighten my load. I nod toward the door, but he glances back at Kismet. Hoping my exit will spur him to follow me, I run out the door with a soul slung haphazardly over my shoulder, bouncing along as I go. I can only hope I'm not causing her more pain. The temperature in the hall is noticeably hotter than it was when we went in.

"Trial by fire," I say to myself, but I can't even hear my own voice over the alarm.

I turn in the direction of the exit, but just as I'm about to start all-out running, Penn runs past me at an inhuman speed with a soul bent over each shoulder. I'm scrambling to keep up with him as a roar sounds over my free shoulder, making me look behind.

A wall of fire licks at our heels and catches my dress. I resist the urge to stop and put it out. The flames kiss my legs, making them move faster toward the exit as Penn runs ahead of me.

He turns and shouts something at me, but I can't hear him over the roar of the flames.

Just as I think the pain is too intense for me to continue, I finally see the gate. *Only a little bit farther,* I think to myself. I clutch the soul I freed, taking comfort from her, knowing I have to survive this, not only for me, but also for her. The entire bottom of my dress is gone, and I use my free hand to slap at it in a vain attempt to stop the flames from climbing higher.

We don't encounter any demons on the way out. They know the flames will destroy any intruders, so they're not worried. Although a part of me is surprised they're not here to watch us burn for sport...

Perhaps the flames are too hot, even for the demons of hell.

Penn throws his body into the gate, and it gives beneath his weight. We tumble out into the clouds and he kicks it shut behind us with his foot, sealing the Cleanse behind the huge black gate of hell.

The flames extinguish as soon as my body hits the clouds, and for a few moments, we all just lay where we are, breathing in huge gulps of air. Pain radiates throughout my body.

I try to move, but I find it too difficult. I want to make sure the souls we carried out with us are okay, but I can't bring myself to even turn my head.

"Michaela," Penn says, but his voice sounds distant. I try to answer him, but it comes out as a moan.

He scoops me up, prompting even more pain, and I cry out.

"I'm sorry," he says. "Stay with me. I'll get you to a healer."

"The souls."

"They are fine. They're safe. We did it."

We must've looked like quite the spectacle as he ran with my half-naked body through the heavens. I don't remember much of the trip to the healers.

When I wake up, my body feels completely refreshed in a way I haven't experienced in weeks. But my mind is still in too much of a fog for me to put the pieces together.

Galenia is in my room. Why isn't she working? Horatia is there too. And Penn. And Webber. They found him. He's okay.

Despite the way Webber's avoiding eye contact and crossing his arms over his chest, I feel like I could hug him.

"Webber. You're safe," I croak out. The sound of my voice surprises me. It's rough from disuse.

He reluctantly turns to me and nods, a grim expression on his face.

It brings all the memories screaming back to me. The prison. The Cleanse. Lily.

Suddenly frantic, I sit up in bed. "How much time has passed? Did they take Lily?"

"No. They're still expecting you to do it. You were supposed to take her yesterday, but you weren't really prepared to do that," Penn explains. "They've pulled some strings and the girl is in a coma, waiting for you. Your boss came to see you, and the healers assured him you would be healthy enough to work in the morning."

"Ryker was here?" Panic sets in as I swing my legs over the edge of the bed and get up. "Did he see you, Penn?" I ask as I pace the room. "Does he know what we did?"

"He did see me. But he didn't seem to recognize me. Or if he did, he looked the other way. He does know you took an unauthorized trip into hell, but I'm not convinced he knows why. Once we got them out of hell, the souls were kept very secret, under lock and key. But I do believe he intends to speak with you about the whole thing later," Penn answered.

My eyes dart back and forth as I stare at the ground of the healing room, as if I might find answers to all my questions written there.

"But he still wants *me* to collect Lily?"

"Yes. That much was clear," Galenia said. "I was here when he came to visit. He was explicit on that point."

"I wonder why."

"I think he trusts you more than the other Reapers," she offered.

I walk to the window, considering everything that had happened—all we'd accomplished and all we hadn't. The galaxies outside the floor-to-ceiling windows are an awe-inspiring view for me to watch, complete with shooting stars streaking past us.

"The souls," I say into the window, wondering what happened to them. Were they too far gone, or did they make it to heaven?

"They spent some time here with the healers, and the one you carried out is still here. She was in pretty bad condition. They said if we hadn't gotten her out right then, she would've disappeared like the others. She'll join the other two in heaven today, I think."

"Are the Archangels going to take her there themselves? I don't want them to end up in that... in that place again." My questions come out in rapid-fire succession. Penn walks up behind me and puts his hand on my shoulder, trying to calm me. I turn, falling into his open arms.

"They're okay. They let Galenia and Horatia watch them go to heaven."

"It was beautiful," Galenia says through shining eyes. "A host of angels welcomed them, singing joyful songs."

I take a deep breath. They are safe. After a few beats, I pull back from him. "We survived the Cleanse, Penn."

"I know," he says. "I didn't intend to cease existing in that place."

"When I saw you trying to free Kismet, I wasn't so sure."

He frowns and looks away.

"I'm sorry," I say, immediately regretting I've reminded him that she's still in there. "We *will* get her out. I promise."

"Why are you so sure she's still in there? Wouldn't the Cleanse kill her?" He seems despondent, and now I know why. He thinks we've failed them.

"No. Penn, oh my gosh, no. The Cleanse only burns intruders. They would've been left untouched. If they aren't there by the time we get back, it's because we took too long, not because they burned in the Cleanse. We *will* get her and Andrew out of there."

"Or die trying," he said quietly.

"Hell hasn't killed me yet."

There's a look of such desperation and vulnerability on his face. Before I know it, he's scooped me back into his arms and is holding me so tightly that I can't breathe.

Galenia and Horatia walk over to join us, and soon, their warm arms are wrapped around us too. Webber just looks on, maintaining his uncomfortable stance and watching us from the corner of his eye.

"We won't fail them. They're your greatest creations," I say quietly, reassuring myself as much as the others.

Penn brings his hand up to my head and smooths my hair. "We only fail if we give up."

SEVENTEEN

The next day, I'm released first thing. As I get out of bed to meet with Ryker before starting my day, I can't help but hear Penn's words in my head. *We only fail if we give up.* He's right. Even if we only save one of them in the end, it's better than abandoning them all to their fate, right?

Ryker's office is situated between the naming room and the gate leading outside. I walk to it cautiously, not sure what to expect. What can I say to him? I have no apologies to make for my actions last night, particularly since God seemed to encourage me.

I knock tentatively on his door, and he responds immediately. "Come in." Even through the door, his deep voice rings loud and clear.

"You wanted to see me?" I smooth my brand-new dress as I walk into his office. The healers did amazing work; there aren't any scratches on my knees and my burns are completely healed. The only wounds that remain are the ones on my heart.

He gestures toward the plush black velvet armchair across from his white desk. The entire office is decorated in black and white. The cupboards are black, the flooring is white, the art on the wall is black and white, and even his accessories match the décor. It doesn't surprise me. The entire wing is decorated like that.

"You're looking better."

"Thank you." I deliberately keep my answer short, not sure where he's going with this.

"First, I want to talk business with you. Just so you know, we'll be relocating any dissenters who continue to refuse to work."

I frown. I've been expecting this. The only reason the punishment didn't come sooner is because there was a group of them, and we are so short handed. Still, I'm surprised by the leniency of the punishment.

"Relocation?" I pry.

"Yes. Until we can agree on a consequence for their actions, we can't have them idly sitting around the heavens. We need workers. And there is some disagreement as to an appropriate punishment. When the vote is unanimous, sentences will be served. If necessary, God will lay down the final vote, but we've been given some time to resolve the issue on our own," he explains.

I nod. Division among the heavens must mean some of the heavenly beings in charge want the dissenters eliminated, and some don't. It seems harsh, but after what I've seen and been through, I get it.

"I understand," is all I can think to say.

He looks at me with a kindness he doesn't often reveal. "I'm sure you do." As he clears his throat, his stern expression returns. "We've managed to get a handful of new recruits from higher up, but it wasn't easy. Now, we're working hard to get them on the fast track, but for the time being, it'll be tight."

My frown deepens as I consider how long it takes to get recruits—we only get a new Reaper maybe twice a decade to help with the rate of population growth on Earth and account for the occasional retirement—so serious exceptions have been made for us. Even so, it takes considerable time to train recruits. There are manuals to study, tests to pass, tours to take, and mentoring. I haven't even been assigned a recruit as far as I know. There's no possible way they'll be ready for the field any time soon.

"In fact, I think you'll be happy to learn that I've put Miette in charge of training them. She has a good heart. I think it will be a good experience for her."

I smile, in spite of the circumstances. My shy friend will have to come out of her shell now.

"There's something else. We've devised a way for the Reapers in the field to shield themselves from the ghosts."

"The others have been told about this?"

"Yes."

He goes through the details with me, and it seems pretty simple. *Think of your assignment, and only your assignment. Surround yourself with the soul's energy.* Additionally, we'll be given more information about each assignment to read over, and short clips of their life will play as we walk through the mists to retrieve them. It will take longer to do each job, but it'll be safer. And I like the idea of learning more about the people we take home. It will help us make a deeper connection with them.

"You know, this approach might actually be helpful in other ways. They might come with us faster if they're more comfortable."

He smiles at me; it's a tired smile, but it's a smile nonetheless. "And that's why I like you. You take these changes in stride, always looking for the positive. Michaela, I rely heavily on you. You are one of my most trusted Reapers, perhaps my most valuable." He leans forward on his desk, resting his elbows on the top, and intertwines his fingers. "In short, I need your help."

"Thank you, sir. That's very kind of you." I shift uncomfortably, waiting for what's to come.

"I have a feeling the incident in hell had something to do with the surprises. Although you're usually a follower of the rules, I also know you're not the type to sit by idly as the world falls to pieces around you. You know more than you're letting on."

Clearing my throat, I avoid eye contact with him.

"Yes, well. I just wanted to tell you to be careful. We'd be lost without you."

His deep brown eyes are clouded with concern when I finally meet them. I open my mouth to speak, but the words don't form, so I close it again and lean back in the chair, totally at a loss. It's the furthest thing from what I expected him to say. The reprimand I was expecting ended up taking the form of praise.

"Thank you, sir," I manage to squeak out while I look at a particularly interesting hangnail on my index finger.

"Thank you and…" He waits for me to fill in the blank, but I'm not sure what he wants. I can't promise him anything.

He sighs heavily. "And you'll be careful?" he finally adds.

I nod quickly. "I will be careful. I *am* being careful."

"If those burns were a result of you being careful, I'd hate to see you being reckless."

A smile cracks my face in what feels like the first time in days. It feels good. "Me too, sir. Me too."

"You'll be easing back into your workday with just the one name. As we did yesterday while you were recovering, we divvied your daily allotment of 2,500 souls among the remaining reapers. Those who've stayed with us have been very devout and pulling long hours into the night to make up the work. They're all pulling for you, Michaela. None of us want you overdoing it today." He looks hard at me, and I nod, letting him know I understand. "Now, get to work," he says as he leans back in his chair and shifts his attention to the holographic screen off to the side. To me, it displays a beautiful tropical beach, but I'm sure he sees something else entirely. Security in the heavens isn't top of the line for nothing. And yet, evil has still found its way in.

I stand to go, but he stops me before I'm out the door. "Michaela, one more thing."

As I turn to face him, standing half in and half out of his office, he says, "Good luck today. I know this won't be easy."

I nod. "Thank you," I say. And then I close the door behind me.

I walk to the door without stopping in the naming room. I have my name. It's all I hope to accomplish today. I don't need to get riled by the other Reapers, the dissenters who refuse to work. I don't need to see the terrified faces of the ones who *are* still working, knowing what we're walking into, despite the supposed safety measures in place. We're the ones testing those measures after all. No. I don't need to think about all that. All I need is Lily.

So I walk back into the mists, thinking only of her.

The safety measures Ryker and his team developed work brilliantly. The ghosts don't come near me. It's as if I've created a bubble made of thoughts of Lily and her family, based on all the memories I watched in the mists as I made my approach. I watched her grow from a bright-eyed, curly-haired little spitfire to a total teenaged handful. But it's clear her parents love her, and she loves them back. Ryker was right. This won't be easy.

Then I spot Wyatt leaning against the wall in the hallway outside Lily's hospital room. He smiles, although I can't see it through his shaggy beard.

I want to hug him, but I know our worlds can't collide that way.

He walks over, hands in his pockets, and nods at me.

"Wyatt. So nice to see you. What are you doing here in New York?"

"Had a visit yesterday from a fella named Ryker."

"Oh?" I ask.

"Scared the dickens outta me to be honest. Thought he was comin' for me."

I laugh. It feels good. I need this before I take this child's soul.

"He told me you might need some extra help today. That this girl's special."

"She is." I glance at the door to her room, behind which I can hear the soft murmurs of her family. Her time is soon, and the thought fills me with sadness.

"Ryker flew me out here at a moment's notice, just to make sure you were able to get your job done." We share a silent moment as I process what he's saying. It's a measure of cooperation the likes of which the heavens and Earth have never seen before. It's both exciting and sad. But really, we *should* be working together to stop this, especially since we now know the criminal is likely human.

Wyatt clears his throat. "It's not all bad. That one over there isn't terrible to look at." He nods toward the waiting area. Fia is sitting in a chair, nursing a cup of coffee. I recognize the striking, grey-eyed woman as Aida, from Penn's description of her. The man sitting next to her can only be Cody, and Eve is sitting between them, totally distraught. I recognize her from Lily's memories. The girls were friends. They *are* friends. I frown and shake my head before retuning my attention to Fia and Wyatt.

"You should talk to her. I think you'd like her."

"You know her?" he asks, a bit of hope in his voice.

"She's a very old friend."

He doesn't ask any more questions, and I know Lily's time is growing short. I frown as I take in the friends and family gathered around this well-loved girl. This isn't right, and yet, here I am, doing it anyway.

Wyatt senses my despair. "I'm sorry."

"Me too." It's good to see him. It gives me the strength to face what's to come.

I round the corner and stand in front of the girl's closed door. In that moment, I turn and catch the eye of the old Fate. She's staring right at me, a look of deep concern on her face. The other people in the waiting room are totally unaware of what's going on around them—they're all silently looking at their phones, talking about what to get for lunch, or simply sitting and staring. None of them notice when Fia stands and walks toward the girl's room, keeping her eyes on me.

Long before Fia can reach me, I cross the threshold into her room. It's time. Fia stops dead and goes to Eve, watching me silently. She knows. I frown and nod at her. She mouths something to me—it looks like, "Stop this," but I can't be sure.

I nod, hoping I caught the old Fate's meaning.

Passing through the closed door, I find Lily's parents sitting on either side of her bed, holding her hands. Her mother, who looks almost exactly like her, reads from a card someone sent to the sick girl. The father is listening as he brushes the hair off his daughter's face.

Later, they will say Lily had a stroke. Something that was lying in wait for the perfect storm of conditions before unleashing itself on her fragile, teenage body.

Her soul looks confused after it detaches.

"Lily," I say to her, hoping to offer some comfort. "I'm here to help."

She glances at me briefly before returning her gaze to her body on the bed. Her parents are staring in horror at the heart monitor as a nurse rushes into the room. Two other nurses pull them away as they get to work on her body. Of course, it's a lost cause—the proof is standing right across from me.

"Lily, come. You don't want to watch this."

Her parents are weeping now, and the look on Lily's face is so beyond desolated when she turns to look at me again.

"What's happening?"

"Nothing I can't save you from." I say, hoping beyond hope that's true.

Lily is reluctant to come with me, and I don't blame her. Nurses and doctors rush into the room. Her parents cling to each other as the monitors scream and alarms wail.

"Why is this happening?" Lily asks.

"I don't know," I answer honestly.

"This isn't right, is it?"

"No. It isn't."

We are silent for a few moments more before she turns to me. Her gray eyes pierce my very existence, breaking my heart more than ever. "Now what?" The statement is heartbreaking in its simplicity. She knows she's lost her life on Earth and can't reclaim it. She's more accepting and mature than most adults I escort to the other side, let alone any of the surprises I've taken up until now.

"Now, I take you home."

"*This* is my home." She looks back at her family with longing in her eyes.

"This was your home. Now, I take you to your new home."

"Without them?"

My breath hitches in my throat as I try to control my emotions. "Without them." It's little more than a whisper, but she nods in acknowledgment.

"I don't like it."

"I don't either."

She looks away from her family and back to me, surprise on her face. "You don't like your job?"

"Sometimes I don't."

She frowns. "So why do it?"

"Because if I don't, you'll become one of them." I nod toward a ghost who happens to be wandering past her room. The doctors threw her door open in their rush to save her, and now we can clearly see him wandering back and forth. He's wailing in grief, but we're the only ones who can hear him. The others in the hall will only feel a slight chill, maybe a prickle on the back of their necks. But they'll never know why.

"He doesn't seem very happy."

"No. He's not. I want you to be happy."

"Then let me stay here... like I was before." Somehow, she knows to make the distinction between staying on Earth as a ghost and staying on Earth as a human. I marvel at this young girl's wisdom.

"It's not that easy," I say sadly. "You've been called home."

She nods, but there's a frown on her face. "So I don't have a choice?"

"There is always a choice. But if you choose to stay, you stay as one of them. If you come with me, your family will join you when the time comes."

Her frown grows deeper as she watches the doorway, as if hoping for another glimpse of the ghost. I know Wyatt is out there, keeping him distracted, so I'm not worried. Still, the ghost seems restless.

"Why is he here?" She asks.

"He's here for me. For *us*. He thinks I can help him get home."

"But you can't?"

"No. If they stay by choice or are left behind, they're here forever."

"That's sad, don't you think?" she asks.

Again, I struggle to control my emotions. "Yes. It *is* sad."

Sighing heavily, she walks closer to her mom. I stay behind, giving her a moment. She places a hand on her mom's back and bends over to whisper in her ear. "I'll miss you."

Her mother lets out a tortured wail, and her dad hugs her close. Lily pulls back in horror. "I can't stay," she says as she backs away from them.

"No. It's not a good idea in most cases."

"Let's go then," she says, turning away from them.

I grab her hand and lead her into the mists. As it closes in around us, I glance over my shoulder one last time at this family that has been shattered by the human who's wreaking such havoc on both of our worlds. How many other lives has she ruined?

"I promise to get to the bottom of this, Lily," I say, knowing she won't fully understand, but needing to say it anyway.

"I believe you." She doesn't demand further explanation, offering simple acceptance instead.

Her memories are all happy and filled with love. Like the memories I saw in the mists on my way to collect Lily, one or two of the memories even feature Eve.

We walk in silence as memories of birthdays, trips to Disney, boys, and more family time play before us. She's had a short life, but there's no denying it's been a good one.

Her final memory is bittersweet. She's about eight, sitting in front of her teacher, listening to her read *Matilda*. It strikes a chord with her, and I can tell she wants to reach people the way Dahl is reaching her. She wants to be a writer. It lights a passion in her that will never come to fruition. It's a little bittersweet for me, knowing that she was meant to become one of the greats, and now she never will.

She frowns and clears her throat, as if trying not to cry.

"Will I see anyone I know? It would be nice to see a familiar face."

"You have lots of familiar faces waiting for you, Lily, including your grandparents. They will welcome you with open arms, sweet child."

The gate of heaven appears before us as the mists clear completely and I walk her to it. We don't speak as we close the distance to her final destination.

"Will you leave me here?" she asks, a hint of fear in her voice. I think of Kismet and Andrew, still trapped in that horrible prison. I won't let that happen to her.

"No. I'll go in with you to make sure you make it home safely."

Thankfully, she doesn't pick up on the ominous nature of my comment, and we walk hand in hand through the gate. To my surprise and gratitude, there are two Archangels waiting for us. They're a bit intimidating, and Lily stops short of them. Their white robes flow behind them, and their enormous white wings cast a shadow over us. But their welcoming smiles and open arms belie their fierce beauty. Lily and I take a step toward them. Then something inexplicable happens. Someone puts a hand on each of the angels' shoulders, and their smiles fade as they disappear right before our eyes.

In their wake, a perfectly average-looking, middle-aged woman appears before us.

A human.

EIGHTEEN

"Michaela. What a pleasure to finally meet you," she says. Her voice is grating; her tone is snarky.

"In order to meet, we both have to know who the other is. That requires you to introduce yourself," I say, positioning myself between her and Lily. I try not to sound as shaken as I feel after watching her… Well, I don't know what she just did, to be honest.

She smiles at me. "That's cute. Almost as cute as you thinking you can save all the souls from my prison." The hate in her voice doesn't belong here at the gates of heaven. How did she do it? "You think you can protect her?"

She snaps her fingers, and when I turn around, Nathair is behind me, still dressed in the Reaper's uniform, although it feels like a mockery of his former position. The smile that stretches across his face as he grabs Lily tells me he enjoys this work. It makes me think he wasn't kidnapped after all. Or if he was, he's certainly working with this person, this Mara, willingly now.

"Michaela! Help!"

"I'm trying! Don't panic. Everything will be okay," I assure her… and myself. I glance back and forth between my two adversaries, defensively holding my hands out. I have never seen an Archangel defeated before, but I struggle to keep my fears of this woman at bay. Lily needs me.

"Yes. Everything *will* be okay," the human says. "For my son, Shiloh."

I'm feeling like I'm twenty steps behind her, and I'll never catch up. "What?"

"My name is Mara." But of course, I already know that. "You're going to help me save him. Whether you want to help or not."

She raises her hands, and the world around me goes black as I feel myself collapsing to the ground.

Names

Aida: Helper. Cody's wife, mother to Eve.

Alvin: Wise. Old man Michaela takes.

Amiee: Beloved. The wife of the old man who Michaela takes.

Andrew: Warrior or strength. Kismet's true love.

Ariel: Angel of protection. Reaper that Michaela idly chats with before their morning meeting.

Audrey: Strength. Woman Michaela takes.

Cody: Helpful. Aida's husband, who helps Penn out of the swamp.

Daevas: Demon. One of the demons who nearly finds Michaela.

Dempsey: Proud. The first man Michaela takes in the book.

Eve: Lively or life. Cody and Aida's oldest (and first) daughter.

Fia: Weaver. The woman that Penn replaced as Spinner.

Galenia: Small and intelligent. The third Fate who decides how a life will end.

Heth: Trembling fear. Michaela's enemy, instigator among the Reapers.

Horatia: Timekeeper. The second Fate who decides how long a life will be.

Irene: Peaceful. Woman Michaela takes.

Jeff: Divinely peaceful. Second name on the list of surprises.

Kismet: Destiny. Andrew's true love.

Lily: Pure. Child Michaela is assigned to take, and the last surprise.

Mara: Bitter. The human.

Michaela: Feminine of Michael, the angel of death. The Reaper.

Miette: Small sweet thing. Michaela's reaper friend.

Morfran: Celtic word for a mythical and particularly ugly demon. One of the demons they encounter in hell.

Nathair: Snake. Reaper who's on leave/missing.

Nysa: New beginning. The first surprise name, the first to have her thread cut short.

Penn: Masculine form of Penelope, meaning Weaver. First of the three Fates, the Spinner.

Ryker: Strength. Reaper's boss.

Shiloh: Shiloh was where a critical battle took place during the American Civil War. Additionally, the Hebrew translation of this word is 'the one to whom it belongs.' Shiloh is the human's—Mara's—child.

Sophia: Wisdom. Reaper who asks how they know for sure they're not in danger.

Wyatt: Guide. Ghost hunter who saves Michaela.

Webber: Weaver. Penn's rival who's promoted to Spinner when Penn is banished.

Meanings found using basic Google searches and MeaningofNames.com

Did you enjoy this book?
Be sure and leave a review!

ACKNOWLEDGEMENTS

This book was certainly a labor of love, weighing heavily on the labor part. Ha! Even after eight books, I still fight with them sometimes. Because of that, I am so grateful for everyone in my life who supports me as I pursue my passion.

First of all, all thanks go to God. Every book I write, I am amazed by my blessings, and this book is no different. I am eternally grateful for the time and finances to be able to do what I love.

My husband was a huge player in this one, helping me decide the best path for not only this book, but also The Human (book 3 in this series). He is the logic to my emotion, and it was just what I needed to see this project through to the end.

Special thanks to my amazing team this time. My cover designer, Robert, is doing awesome things with these books, and I'm so proud to have him with us! Angela, man, did we work hard on this one! Thank you so much for sticking with me through my indecision about it. And Cynthia, what can I say? You know exactly how to make a great book Amazing with a capital A. It's because of you I have readers coming to me saying they love my books because they never find errors in them.

Of course, my parents are always staunch supporters, and thank you seems inadequate for them. They're always there when I feel like I have to give up, start over, or try something else. They never tell me what to do—okay, that's a lie. They always tell me what to do, but if I don't listen, they respect my decisions. It's an amazing quality I hope I can show my own daughter when the time comes.

My friends, Mary, Dannie, and Christian. You guys are what amazing is made of. Without you, I wouldn't know what true friendship looked like, and for that, I thank you.

And finally, you dear reader. I know how much time it takes to read a book. I know you've chosen to spend that time with me instead of your family, or working, or exercising, or any other hundreds of tasks on your to-do list. And I'm so glad you did. I can't wait to see you again in June. Until then,

—S

ABOUT THE AUTHOR

Stephanie Erickson is an English Literature graduate from Flagler College. She lives in Florida with her family. The Reaper is her eighth novel.

She loves to connect with readers! Follow her on Facebook at http://www.facebook.com/stephmerickson, Twitter @sm_erickson, or stop by her Web site at www.stephanieerickson-books.com.

You can also get the latest news on new releases, contests, and author appearances by signing up for her newsletter on her Web site.

STEPHANIE'S BOOKS

Standalones:
The Blackout
The Cure

The Unseen Trilogy:
Unseen
Unforgiven
Undivided

The Dead Room Trilogy:
The Dead Room

The Children of Wisdom:
The Fate
The Reaper
The Human: Coming May 2016

Printed in Great Britain
by Amazon